THE INVENTOR

•

•   •

W. E. GUTMAN

CCB Publishing
British Columbia, Canada

The Inventor

Copyright ©2009 by W. E. Gutman
ISBN-13   978-1-926585-75-8
First Edition

Library and Archives Canada Cataloguing in Publication

Gutman, W. E., 1937-
The inventor / written by W. E. Gutman.
Includes bibliographical references.
ISBN 978-1-926585-75-8
I. Title.
PS3607.U86I59 2010   813'.6   C2010-900697-6

Original art: **The Ship of Fools**, by Hieronymus Bosch, Musée du Louvre, Paris. Cover design by the author.

This book is printed on acid-free paper.

References to real persons, alive or deceased, and allusions to verifiable historical incidents are meant to lend the narrative epic realism. All other characters and events are fictitious and any similarity to real persons, living or dead is purely coincidental. Inferences and speculations readers may draw from this work are entirely their own.

Publisher: CCB Publishing
             British Columbia, Canada
             www.ccbpublishing.com

FOR THE WIDOW'S SON,
AND IN DEFENSE
OF REASON

Also by W. E. Gutman:

Journey To Xibalba -- THE SUBVERSION OF HUMAN
RIGHTS IN CENTRAL AMERICA. © 2000. Reporter's
Notebook (out of print).

NOCTURNES -- *Tales From The Dreamtime.*
© 2006. Fiction (ISBN 1-4259-5951-2)

ADRIFT --- Life In Transit. © 2008.
Autobiography (ISBN 13 978-0-9810246-9-1)

Flight From Ein Sof. © 2009.
Fiction (ISBN 13-978-1-926585-17-8)

CONTENTS

PROLOGUE

ICHEL MONTVERT loves books. He was six or seven when he first leafed through an art album he had casually pulled off a shelf at home. With the old Blaupunkt radio humming in the background, he sat crossed-legged on a fading Persian rug, the large tome stretching across his lap. He would forever be transformed by the experience.

"They were all there," Montvert told me years later as we dined at Jo Goldenberg's on Rue des Rosiers in Paris. "Titian. Botticelli. Michelangelo. Rembrandt. Van Eyck. Van Gogh. Corot. Gainsborough. Turner. Toulouse-Lautrec. Utrillo. Gauguin. Degas. Renoir. Monet. Cézanne. I couldn't get enough. I was seduced by the interplay of light and color, awed by motion so deftly captured and frozen in space, inveigled by the lyricism and gauzy quality of impressionism, the precision of neo-Classicism, the refinement of the Venetian School, the probing intensity of portraiture."

There was one artist he kept revisiting, and one painting in particular among several strange works by an old master whose name meant nothing to Montvert at the time. Nor did the mysterious and exotic title of a legendary masterwork he found himself staring at and dissecting inch by inch for hours on end.

"I was only a kid but I sensed that, unlike the other painters, this artist didn't just replicate life. He imagined it, fabricated it, refashioned it, upended it," Montvert had exclaimed, glints of childlike wonderment flickering in his eyes.

"Set against gossamer landscapes and improbable perspectives, his images seem to jump out of their two-dimensional plane, splashing the optic nerve with exquisite melancholy, dotting his universe with things and creatures that nature, in its infinite wisdom, or utter lack of imagination, has chosen not to sire. Here you find monsters and mutants and grotesque hybrids. There you come face to face with warlocks and grimacing witches frolicking among aimless throngs given to paroxysms of elation or stricken with catatonic stupor. Encoded in the language of allegory and symbolism but crafted to bare enduring truths, his paintings said more than they implied. They seemed to be speaking to me with an intimacy that was both comforting and terrifying. I let my eyes be seduced and my eyes wandered, seeking to be challenged as they were being dazzled. In a way I could not fully process at the time, I was also stirred by their eroticism, which I found more beguiling than the prosaic photos I sneaked a peek at in my father's medical books."

What Montvert finally grasped when, as an art student, he rediscovered his childhood idol, was that in his company he had been treated all along to a vivid and eloquent articulation of the idiom of conflict.

"The seemingly mismatched details he crams into his paintings are like pieces of a puzzle," he explained. "You can ponder each one individually and miss the big picture, or you can bring them together into a congruent whole that delivers the artist's central message: Life is a journey across a minefield of ceaseless friction. Resentment spawns hostility. Envy elicits malice. Ignorance leads to rigid thinking. Fixed ideas breed suspicion. Greed, narcissism, scorching ambition and uncontrollable lust inspire violence."

●

● ●

Conflict is not only elemental; it is essential to life. Evolution of the species is driven by conflict and sustained by adaptation to the stresses it creates and the torments it inflicts. The clash of egos, the spark that ignites passions and deepens the ideological divide between men, leads to a more sinister form of conflict because the irreconcilable beliefs, opinions and value systems that trigger hostility are imparted, not inborn. It was Sigmund Freud who postulated the now widely accepted theory that we are the product of our subconscious. Freud was careful to add that the subconscious is neither amorphous nor indelible, but rather the aggregate of myriad post-natal influences and coercions. The psyche is fashioned, transformed and often fouled by early childhood experiences and warped by brainwashing -- the planting of preset ideas -- a technique parents, teachers, clergy and other public custodians whose authority we are taught never to question or defy apply with ferocious conviction.

As children we eagerly swallow the "truths" these figureheads concoct to beguile or entrap us, from Santa Claus to the boogey man and the tooth fairy, from the supernatural *übermensch* who can part oceans, rain fire and spread pestilence and famine, to the "immaculate" birth of a virgin who, visited by "angels" bears a man-God whose recondite pronouncements -- if his biographers are to be trusted -- are conflated into a cult some 300 years after his preordained death, miraculous "resurrection" and subsequent ascension to "heaven."

Then one day, by word of mouth or the emergence of nascent intelligence, we learn that the pixies and the elves that kindled our imagination and the ogres that populated our nightmares are myth and fraud, as are their principal agents -- our parents. With careful programming, which includes crafty counsel not to wander beyond the limits of time-honored "realities," we enter adulthood conditioned to accept and encouraged to disseminate other absurdities that owe their being and their irritating persistence to the constant drumbeat of political and religious indoctrination.

No one is "born" a believer or an atheist. No one spurts out of the womb a Jew, Baptist or Muslim, a Liberal or Conservative, a chauvinist or a freethinker. We all come into this world with a blank slate. Parental propaganda, our social climate and assorted constraints mold us into cookie-cutter replicas of our devoted retrofitters. We are all endowed with a brain capable of discerning the truth but we are by now so emotionally mangled by encoding and spellbound by the rote repetition of sanctioned doctrine that we submit to mindless, synchronized rituals alleged to benefit "society." To survive, the conjurer, the master of doublespeak -- religion -- must cling to fictions that do not exist in the pristine vacuum of an untainted mind but are planted there so they may sprout, tentacle-like, the better to strangle reason.

Held in check, redirected away from prefabricated truths, conflict can bring down the curtains of ignorance and shed light where there is none. It can help change minds, alter perceptions. *I think, therefore I doubt*, replaces the *credo* of inflexible dogma. Skepticism in the absence of provable fact has not only propelled science to its phenomenal heights, it has also freed minds trapped in ideological warrens from which knowledge, logic and enlightenment are kept out.

Where does fiction end and fact begin? Do the two ever intersect at a point where reality, improbability and inevitability coexist? Can conflict engender a hyper-reality in which are found the truths that craven men fear to know and cautious men fear to tell? In the perfect geometry of coincidence, will these truths assume an aura of frightening plausibility?

Knowing others is wisdom.
Knowing oneself is enlightenment.
Lao Tzu (circa 500 BCE)

I call degenerate practices and senseless
beliefs diseases of humanity.
Maimonides (1135-1204)

Men never do evil so completely and cheerfully as
when they do it from religious convictions.
Blaise Pascal (1623-1662)

"Religion is a system of superstition that produces
fanatics and serves the purposes of despotism."
Thomas Paine (1737-1809)

Religion promotes and/or exploits personal guilt.
What people who clamor that society needs religion
really mean is that we need police.
H. L. Mencken (1880-1956)

God and country are an unbearable team;
they break all records for oppression and bloodshed.
Luis Buñuel (1900-1983)

Lies are fascinating for what they reveal about the liar.
Federico Fellini (1920-1993)

Isn't it enough to see that a garden is beautiful
without having to believe that
there are fairies at the bottom of it?
Douglas Adams (1952-2001)

Sell the Vatican and feed the poor.
Sarah Silverman (2008)

To catch a glimpse of the evil in Man,
one must first peel off the outer layers of piety.
Itamar Sittenfeld (2009)

NARRAGONIA

O N PERMANENT DISPLAY at the Musée du Louvre in Paris is an oil painting on wood of very modest dimensions, approximately twenty-three inches high and thirteen inches wide. A work of nervous energy that captures the tormented expressions of its characters, the painting lampoons the credulity of the masses and warns against the greed, decadence and hypocrisy of the clergy. Perhaps inspired by Sebastian Brant's moralistic poem, *Das Narrenschiff,* the painting is known as *La Nef des Fous* or *The Ship of Fools.* Dense in symbolism, it is one of the 15th century's most inscrutable works or art.

Brant, a humanist and a contemporary of the painter, tells the story of a craft laden with fools and steered by fools sailing toward a fools' paradise, *Narragonia.* The ship is a metaphor for life and *Narragonia* a satirical emblem for a world gone mad. Written in 1494, two years after Columbus' first voyage to the "Indies," the poem attacks the failings and extravagances of his age. No folly is left uncensored as it lashes unsparingly at the hydra of popery, the parasitic idleness of monasticism and the perfidy of false piety.

In his groundbreaking *Madness and Civilization,* French philosopher and historian Michel Foucault writes about the ancient practice of "shanghaiing" the "insane" (and other pariahs) and forcing them to serve as crew on ocean-going vessels. Penned by a noted New York psychiatrist, the late Dr. José Barchilon, the introduction to Foucault's book relates how

"Renaissance men developed a delightful, yet horrible way of dealing with their mad denizens: they were put on a ship and entrusted to mariners because folly, water and sea, as everyone then 'knew,' had an affinity for each other. Thus, 'ships of fools' criss-crossed the seas, oceans and canals of Europe with their comic and pathetic cargo of souls. Some of them found pleasure and even a cure in the changing surroundings, in the isolation of being cast off, while others withdrew further, became worse or died alone and away from their families. The cities and villages which had thus rid themselves of their crazed and crazy could now take pleasure in watching the exciting sideshow when a ship full of foreign lunatics would dock at their harbors."

In his book, Foucault examines the ideas, practices, institutions, art and literature relating to madness in Western history. He begins with the middle Ages, noting the social and physical alienation of lepers, and argues that with the gradual disappearance of leprosy, madness replaced the dreaded and disfiguring disease in the public's perception, hence the practice of sending mad people away on long-distance ships. During the Renaissance, madness came to be regarded not as a consequence of impiety but as an omnipresent disorder brought on by man's obsessive search for God. It was also thought to signify the limits of social order and point to a deeper truth. A century later, insanity was regarded as the obverse of common sense, as the inability (or unwillingness) to reason. The mad had lost, or surrendered what made them human; they had become animal-like and were treated as such. It took another 100 years for insanity to be regarded as an illness that must be treated.

Like Brant, the painter of *The Ship of Fools* attacks with biting wit the weaknesses, ideological deformities and vices of his time. He aims his sharpest barbs at the Church.

Whatever the source of the work might have been, the painting beckons us aboard an overloaded craft brimming with wantonness and psychosis. Hugging the shore, its course unknown, with nary a wharf in sight, it drifts on currents of metaphor and dark premonitions. Madness spares no one, least of all the clergy and its compliant flock. The waters are opaque and congealed, clearer at the far end of an inhospitable coastline. A leafy barrier rises from an inaccessible beach.

Eight travelers huddle in the narrow boat. Another is perched on a tree branch grafted into the hull. Two more wade in the water, another emerges from a hedge. Emaciated or grotesquely bloated, their faces express mulishness and angst. In a scene rife with sexual over-tones, a Franciscan friar and a nun who plays the lute, a symbol of eroticism (as are the luscious cherries scattered on a makeshift table) are poised to take a bite out of a loaf of corn bread hanging from a string. Leaning on the prow, another nun clutches a pitcher, an allusion to her sex, as she pesters a man holding a large glass container, also a phallic symbol. Hunched over the stern, a man retches convulsively. More than the consequence of intemperance or debauchery, his queasiness is the first echo of the terrible nausea that grips the damned. It also diagnoses the early symptoms of the diabolical disintegration of the spirit.

The two men in the water are naked. Are they enjoying a swim or are they immersed in ritual purification? Brandishing a knife, a phallic symbol, a rapscallion roosting in the boughs, attempts to cut the thread that ties a fried chicken, or swan, to a mast from which flutters a banner decorated with a crescent-moon, a symbol of lunacy.

The oddest character, perhaps the most noteworthy, is the hunchback astride a three-pronged tree stump: He is *The Fool*, the twenty-second card of the Tarot, and he represents the highest degree of initiation into the hermetic sciences. He is the ninth voyager, with nine being both the universal integer (the sum of any number multiplied by nine equals nine) and a symbol of regeneration. Turning his back on madness, he drinks from a chalice. Two horns protrude from his hood. With his left hand, he clasps a pole from which dangles the head of a nun or witch. The fluttering fringes of his tunic accentuate his agility and cunning.

In an article published in the *Revue des Arts Initiatiques*, Michel Montvert, a noted art historian and Surrealism expert says there is little doubt that

"The artist, in his quest to exhume and explore the subconscious, encourages creative minds to seek intellectual independence in the pursuit of free thought. Modern surrealism has inherited, or perhaps wrenched, from him its ingenuity and irreverence. But whereas the Moderns deform or upend reality to convey abstract concepts, the author of this disquieting painting draws from Apocalypse, alchemy and the demonic realm of fiends -- real and imaginary -- to expose the iniquities of his time. Through them he expresses profound pessimism about the fate of man.

"A youthful work, the diminutive Ship of Fools is filled with secret language and nuances that invite endless interpretations. We know that the master painter served two patrons: the Church, in conventional religious iconographies; and, with palpable relish, radical adversaries who fought against the Church's despotism and immorality. The very complexity of his haunting renderings has denied us a clear understanding of the mood, feelings and insights that fed them."

Unanticipated circumstances would soon bring the great artist out of the fog of time and, for a brief period of friction and discord, into the glare of public scrutiny. Heretofore the subject of scholarly speculations, the remote and once two-dimensional medieval artist would reach beyond the grave, show his face and bare his soul. The chain of events that ensued would shed new light on his generation. It would also say infinitely more about

the dissonance of our own age and the one-way journey
to the fool's paradises on which many are embarked.

A BLUEBLOOD AND A COMMONER

MAN IS FATED, through evolution and personal initiative, to transit from an artificially imprinted belief in invisible gods and inaccessible spirit forces to the positive stages of existence, with life being its own justification and reward. Some men rise to the challenge. Others get stuck along the way.

In early January 2008, lured by an irresistible calling and following brilliant seminary studies, 26-year-old Hubert François de Ravaillac, of noble French ancestry, takes the sacred vows and enters the priesthood. He is ordained by Bishop Jean-Marie Touvier at the Eglise Saint-Germain-des-Prés, an 11th century church that rises proud in its austere architectural simplicity in the heart of Paris.

Outside, on the windswept church esplanade, Gypsies, some with infants at their breast, beg for alms. Defying the cold, jugglers and balladeers seek in the goodwill of passersby a chance for recognition, perhaps fame, or perhaps just enough loose change to pay for a warm meal before dark. Across the street, patrons at Les Deux Magots Café sip hot fragrant espressos in thimble-sized cups and cool pale white wines in fluted glasses. In their chairs had once lingered such rabble-rousers as Ernest Hemingway and Gertrude Stein, Samuel Becket and F. Scott Fitzgerald, Aldous Huxley and James Baldwin, Jean-Paul Sartre and Simone de Beauvoir, Picasso and Albert Camus, to name a few. Paris the enchantress had seduced them all.

As these worldly diversions take place in a universe he will forever shun, Hubert François de Ravaillac, prostrate and cross-like on the cold stone floor at the foot of the altar, pledges to consecrate his life to God and his Son Jesus Christ. The oath includes the solemn vow to protect the Church from scandal, at the peril of his own life.

De Ravaillac is a devout Catholic but pastoral service, he believes, should transcend routine priestly occupations. A blueblood, a hereditary anti-communist and a self-flogging zealot who still blames the Jews for the crucifixion of his Savior, the young priest has ceded his mortal body and consecrated his eternal soul to the Holy Church. His mission, as he sees it, and as his superiors in Paris and Rome have noted with cautious interest, is to help steer Roman Catholicism back to the pinnacles of power and prominence it once enjoyed. To do so quietly and with the greatest efficacy, he joins Opus Dei (God's Work), a fabulously rich, aggressively right-wing cloak-and-dagger Catholic organization that wields powers infinitely greater than the imaginary ones the Church ascribes to its favorite scapegoats, the Jews, the Freemasons and the Socialists.

•

•   •

On that same blustery winter morning, Michel Montvert studies the late Chilean painter Roberto Matta's *"psychoanalytic views of the mind,"* his esoteric *"landscapes of the soul."* Matta, a Socialist, believed art, music and poetry have the power to change the lives of people. Montvert, a humanist in an age of declining humaneness, believes that only when freed from adversity, want and suffocating ideologies will people partake of art's enticing fruits.

Unlike de Ravaillac, Montvert comes from a culture where the word God was never uttered -- except as a reflex expletive -- and death or the hereafter had no place at the dinner-table, either in a mystical or existential context. He was never given a religious education, nor deprived of such, and the notion of an invisible, omnipotent creator/arbiter/destroyer seemed ludicrous to him even as a boy. By the time he was old enough to contemplate the enormity of his parents' suffering, especially during the German occupation of France, their indifference to religion had turned to embittered agnosticism -- his father's early childhood religious upbringing and his mother's genteel, pseudo-assimilation into a Christian mainstream notwith-standing. Struck with pancreatic cancer, his mother had endured several months of martyrdom and died convinced that religion is a travesty and a fraud. Heartbroken, his father, a physician, grieved at the fragility of the human body and railed against the

9

staggering imperfection of medical science. He spent the rest of his days in the company of a cantankerous cat mourning his wife and perusing and annotating the Bible -- the Old Testament (he considered the New Testament a crude fantasy) -- not for inspiration or comfort, but to vilify it, to find the contradictions and highlight the aberrations, to poke a wrathful finger at God's unfathomable cruelty, to denounce man's limitless propensity for evil.

Montvert and his father had often chatted long into the night about religion, not in pursuit of an ideological abode but as an exercise in pure reasoning. They agreed that the underpinnings of religion -- mysticism, the supernatural, the *credo quia absurdum* (I believe *BECAUSE* it is absurd), faith in an invisible entity, the rituals, the taboos, the hellish penalties -- had all been contrived to enslave man, not to liberate him. They acknowledged the simplistic precepts of the "Golden Rule," or Ethic of Reciprocity, present in Judaism, Christianity and Islam (but probably of more ancient Buddhist provenance) yet pointed at man's inclination to ignore it, even violate it, in the name of Yahweh, Theos and Allah. They quoted from Hillel the Elder, the 1st century BCE rabbi who summed up the Torah with the command, *"What is hateful to you do not do to your neighbor."* They read Luke (6:31), which teaches, *"Treat others as you want them to treat you."* Last, they turned to the Koran's lofty counsel, *"No one of you is a believer until he desires for his brother that which he desires for himself."*

But "others," "neighbor" and "brother," they knew, have a parochial meaning that, history has shown, signifies "those of *our* own kind -- *us*, not *them*."

This paradox had been astutely dissected a year earlier by CNN journalist Christiane Amanpour in *God's Warriors: The Clash Between Piety and Politics*. Rebroadcast several times since its first airing, the three-part award-winning documentary offers a disturbing rendering of the three major religions' penchant for violence in the service of deity. It also lays bare their unceasing effort to manipulate civil society through indoctrination, intimidation, civil disobedience and, all else failing, swift, copious bloodshed.

Carried to its extremes, *God's Warriors* had shown, religion is a dangerous eccentricity that will render men insane. Only religious delirium could inspire a Muslim to plot the "honor killing" of his own daughter, or to bomb a disco filled with Jewish youths. Only mystical rapture could lead a self-styled Christian to murder doctors performing legal abortions. Only a Jewish zealot could violate the Torah, slaughter Muslims gathered in prayer in their mosque, torch cars on the Sabbath or assault members of a peaceful Gay Pride parade and threaten violence if the Jerusalem police chief allowed the pageant to proceed.

This is the bare face of religion, Montvert *père et fils* had concluded. This is how religion transforms societies into citadels of intolerance, incubators in which simmers the hatred of "heretics," a one-size-fits-all label that describes those who hold different beliefs or who grant themselves the inalienable right to espouse none. Within that conflict rests the unresolved tension between the command to "love one's enemies" and the equally strong injunction to reject and eradicate any alien or divergent dogma, to the death if necessary. In the final analysis, Montvert father and son had reasoned, neither Jew, nor Christian or Muslim knows which of the two commands to follow at any given time. By attacking "heretics" as tools of Satan, religious fanatics seize the rhetorical high ground and shift the focus from embracing one's fellow man to the escapist option of waging war against an imaginary but prescriptive source of evil.

This catch 22 was the preeminent rationale for a succession of gruesome confrontations: the Crusades, the St. Bartholomew's Day massacre, the Inquisition, the 30-Years War, the centuries-old strife in Northern Ireland, the Armenian and Jewish Holocausts, the Hutu-Tutsi reciprocal slaughter, the Hindu-Moslem-Sikh massacres in India and Kashmir, the bloodbath in Sudan and the cyclic carnage between Shia and Sunni Muslims.

Nor has hatred of "heresy" spared the presumptive self-proclaimed paragon of probity, the United States.

"Behold the proliferating dynasties of Elmer Gantries who are hijacking that nation's psyche (while rifling through its pockets)," Michel Montvert had told me more than once, "and witness the phalanx of rapt soul-robbers whose stated strategy is to infiltrate and exploit the coercive power of government." Montvert was right. Despite its implied but halfhearted tradition of separating church from state, the U.S. never made an honest effort to protect against the intrusion of religion into the body politic. The recent past had seen religion woven more deeply into the fabric of governance than ever before. Although the U.S. Constitution guarantees the non-involvement of government in religion, it has spinelessly failed to hinder religion from muscling in on the affairs of state. Such *laissez-faire*, absent in modern France, Montvert had warned, could lead to theocratic control.

The fundamental weakness of democracy, my old friend had often protested, is that it tolerates in its very bosom the existence and propagation of undemocratic principles. With the right checks and balances, he had argued, and unrelenting vigilance, despotic ideas could be deflected. All would be lost if those who chip away at the civil liberties that democracy grants them are the very people sworn to protect the nation, by example, against the erosion of treasured constitutional rights.

●

● ●

De Ravaillac, like all the self-anointed moralizers who find a haven in Opus Dei, sees no conflict in a Golden Rule that also makes room for the persecution of "heretics." His sadomasochism can be traced to a straitlaced upbringing. He owes his iron will -- or is it his fixation with martyrdom -- to a stoic lot, an ancient family with an emblazoned past, now governed by retired French Navy Commander Clovis Godefroy de Ravaillac, his father -- whom Hubert still calls "sir" -- and his mother, Clothilde Dieudonnée de Ravaillac, a woman of exceptional beauty in her youth, now fending off the ravages of sun and tropics with heavy makeup and triple gins and tonic. Hubert, their only offspring (more by accident than choice) quickly learns to manage the lovelessness of his upper crust milieu "like a man," a lesson further beaten into him with his parents' consent by Jesuit bullies at the Collège Sainte Croix, where his dormant bisexuality is awakened and indulged.

●

● ●

Outside of its own doctrinaire circle of followers and fans, Opus Dei has a dappled reputation, mostly bad. Andrew Greeley, the eminent American Catholic priest, sociologist, journalist and best-selling author, has described it as

"a devious, antidemocratic, reactionary, semi-fascist institution, desperately famished for absolute dominion in the Church and quite possibly very close now to having that power."

Calling the elite group, "authoritarian and power-mad," Greeley warns that

"Opus Dei is an extremely dangerous organization because it appeals to the love of secrecy and the power lust of certain kinds of religious personalities. It may well be the most powerful group in the Church today. It is capable of doing an enormous amount of harm. It ought to be forced out of the shadows or suppressed."

Opus Dei has about one million members worldwide. At least 2,000 are ordained priests. With this international cohort of dedicated warriors, Opus Dei has successfully penetrated schools and universities, banks, publishing firms, television and radio stations, ad agencies and film companies. It has been accused of deceptive and aggressive recruitment practices, including *"love bombing"* -- the deliberate and syrupy show of affection by an individual or group as a tool of conscription or conversion -- and instructing celibate members to form friendships, attend social gatherings and submit written reports on potential converts.

The core precept of Opus Dei is *"to help shape the world in a Catholic manner."* *Helpers* include clergy, captains of industry, high-ranking military officers and government officials. The group *"comes surrounded by a political miasma,"* the British daily, The Guardian, noted recently. The super-stealthy organization was founded just before the Spanish Civil War and blossomed in the halcyon Catholic days of *El Caudillo*, fascist dictator Francisco Franco's "crusade" against the Republican left. When Opus Dei came to prominence in the late 1960s it was because Franco's cabinet included an inordinate number of *Opusdeistas* -- too many to be the result of coincidence.

For Father Hubert, whose passion for Christ calls for no less than the repeal of *Laïcité* -- the scrupulously enforced separation of Church and State in France -- membership in Opus Dei arms him with special and far-reaching powers. But the organization's militancy, in his opinion, does not quite match his own God-driven longing to cleanse the world of heretics and deliver sinful, rudderless humanity, by force if necessary, into Christ's loving arms. He seeks and is granted entry into the Knights of Malta, a closed fraternity of the Roman Catholic Church whose upper tier members are fastidiously aristocratic. De Ravaillac, an extremist whose family tree goes back at least 400 years and which includes a reviled regicide, meets or exceeds the Knights' rigorous standards for admission. They consider him quite a "prize catch."

The 900-year-old organization was formerly known as the Sovereign Military Hospitaller Order of the Saints John of Jerusalem, Rhodes and Malta. Modeled after an ancient group of soldier-monks who massacred "infidels," (Muslims, Jews and Cathars) Knights of Malta, ceremonies and rituals *"inculcate lessons of chivalry and courage, and inspire a militant spirit in opposition to all non-Christian ideologies and powers."* With over 10,000 members in 42 countries, the Knights are influential Vatican surrogates with extensive ties to right-wing intelligence networks.

Originally programmed to be ruthless tactical fighters, later adopting a fiercely anti-communist stance, the Knights were instrumental in the creation of the Central Intelligence Agency. They also took part in U.S. global "black" (covert) operations. The founding fathers of the CIA, William "Wild Bill" Donovan and Allen Dulles, the longest-serving CIA director, were Knights, as were many in the CIA hierarchy, including JFK's director, John McCone and Ronald Reagan's director, William Casey. McCone helped engineer the 1973 military coup against Chile's democratically elected president, Salvador Allende. According to journalist Carl Bernstein, Casey gave Pope John Paul II unparalleled access to CIA intelligence, including data on spy satellites and field operatives.

There is compelling evidence that the Knights of Malta were linked to the "Rat Run," the post-World War II getaway route used by Nazi top brass and death camp "scientists" from defeated Germany to the Americas. These thugs were issued new identities and special credentials that ensured escape from prosecution for crimes against humanity. One of them, Major General Reinhard Gehlen, a devout Catholic and legendary Cold War spymaster, surrendered to the U.S. Army Counter-Intelligence Corps in 1945. Because of his experience and useful contacts in the Soviet Union, he was freed, as were seven of his senior officers, in exchange for their pledge to gather intelligence for the United States. Flown to Washington, Gehlen went to work for Donovan and Dulles, then the Office of Strategic Services station chief in Switzerland. Gehlen handed over the names of several OSS officers who were members of the U.S. Communist Party.

A year later, Gehlen was flown back to Germany where he resumed his spy work, this time as a lackey of the U.S. He set up a dummy organization composed of 350 former German intelligence officers. That number eventually grew to 4,000. For many years, the "V-men," (*V-mann* or *Vertrauensmann* -- trusted man) as they were known, were the eyes and ears of the CIA in Western Europe and the Soviet Bloc during the Cold War. Recruited among men who had as little culture, common sense, objectivity or logic as possible, they were used primarily to maintain surveillance of civilian populations in Germany and occupied countries.

Overall, the Gehlen organization's performance was at best disappointing. One rare successful mission infiltrated some 5,000 anti-communists of Eastern European origin into the Soviet Union and its satellites. These agents were trained at a facility named Oberammergau, site of the yearly staging of one of Hitler's favorite diversions, the unambiguously anti-Semitic Passion Plays. The organization was severely compromised when it was infiltrated by communist moles -- as were the CIA and the British MI6. One of the double-agents was the illustrious Harold "Kim" Philby, spy-extraordinaire who served the communist cause until his death in Moscow in 1988.

Gehlen employed hundreds of "ex-Nazis," among them Alois Brunner, Adolf Eichmann's right-hand-man and commander of the Drancy internment camp near Paris. Brunner was responsible for the slaughter of 140,000 Jews. His death has never been confirmed; he was believed to be still alive in 2007. The CIA turned a blind eye and, owing the exigencies of the Cold War, even took part in some of Gehlen's operations.

Robert Wolfe, historian at the U.S. National Archives wrote that

"U.S. Army intelligence accepted Reinhard Gehlen's offer to furnish alleged expertise on the Red Army -- and was bilked by the many mass murderers he hired."

In appreciation for his work, Gehlen, Hitler's Eastern Front intelligence chief who organized and took part in atrocities against Jews, Gypsies and Slavs, was awarded the Knights of Malta's highest decoration, the Grand Cross of Merit. [In 1988, the American branch of the Knights of Malta pinned the Grand Cross on Ronald Reagan *"for devotion to Christian principles."*] People in Central America still remember Reagan as the man who funneled millions of tax dollars to repressive and often brutal regimes whose U.S.-trained death squads murdered hundreds of thousands of innocent civilians.

One of the Knights of Malta's main spheres of influence is Latin America, where fascists and escaped Nazis were given a warm welcome. The late Chilean strongman, General Augusto Pinochet, a CIA-stooge and convicted human rights violator, was a Knight. So is deposed Peruvian dictator, human rights violator and embezzler, Alberto Fujimori, America's "man in Lima" until his arrest in 2005. So was the late Argentinean president Juan Peron who, recently declassified CIA documents suggest, laundered Nazi gold through the Vatican Bank subsidiary, Banco Ambrosiano, which collapsed in 1982. The Vatican Bank is widely believed to have channeled covert U.S. funds to Poland's Solidarity trade union and transferred laundered money from the illegal sale of arms to Iran to the Contras through Banco Ambrosiano.

The scandal, "characterized by pervasive dishonesty and inordinate secrecy," would prompt Congress to conclude that "a cabal of zealots" (members of Reagan's cabinet, later the Bush-1 administration) violated the

Hughes-Ryan Act and the Boland Amendment by failing to inform congressional intelligence committees about its covert actions in the Middle East and Central America. There are those who wonder to this day why Ronald Reagan wasn't impeached and George H. W. Bush indicted for their approval of black missions.[1]

"After World War II," Roman Catholic writer Penny Lernoux writes in her *People of God*,

> "the Vatican, the OSS, elements of the SS, and various branches of the Sovereign Military Order of Malta joined … to help Nazi war criminals escape.…"

Documents reveal that New York Cardinal Francis Spellman, head of the Knights in the U.S. from the 1940s to the 1960s was directly involved in the 1954 right-wing military coup in Guatemala during which at least 200,000 indigenous Maya were massacred and in which the CIA has acknowledged complicity. [Spellman was also linked to organized crime by his long involvement with Archbishop Paul Macinkus of Chicago, former head of the Vatican Bank, and a suspect in the highly suspicious death of Pope John Paul I a month after his election.]

---

[1] Passed in 1974, the Hughes-Ryan Act requires the president of the United States to report all covert operations of the CIA to at least one Congressional committee. The Boland Amendment was a triad to amendments enacted between 1982 and 1984 aimed at limiting U.S. assistance to the CIA-financed Contras in Nicaragua.

•

• •

Guatemala's reputation as a habitual human rights violator, with "disappearances," torture and wholesale murder topping the list of crimes, is well earned. Although civilian regimes have been in place since 1986, development of a civil society and democratic institutions continues to limp along, stunted by the legacy of a brutal past and further obstructed by a corrupt and apathetic judicial system disinclined to prosecute human rights violators. Gone amok, trained by the U.S. Army School of the Americas (antiseptically rechristened the "Western Hemisphere Institute for Security Cooperation" in 2001) the Guatemalan military, the national police and urban constabularies have repeatedly stained the "Land of Eternal Spring" red with blood.

Who helped bankroll the "Dirty War" in Central America? Benefactors include an oddball assortment of powerful confederates. Among them is Robert Macauley, founder and chairman of AmeriCares, the New Canaan, Connecticut-based disaster relief agency... and the Knights of Malta, the Vatican's mouthpiece, a patron of the CIA and a regular conduit into the Isthmus. Sympathizers and cheerleaders include the once-presidential hopeful, Pat Buchanan, and W. R. Grace Company head, the late J. Peter Grace, a devout Catholic associated with CIA-assisted coups and known to have tried to scuttle progressive international labor movements. Grace, who once referred to former New York Governor Mario Cuomo as a "homo" and former New

York Mayor David Dinkins as a "pinkins," also had a fondness for Nazis. In 1958, he interceded to facilitate the immigration of Dr. Otto Ambros, one of the developers of Zyklon-B gas, used with deadly efficiency in Nazi extermination camps. Convicted at the Nuremberg trials for mass murder and for supplying slave labor, Ambros was later hired by Grace as a consultant. Other leading players in a scenario scripted by the religious right, U.S. spydom and the military, lay bare the magnitude of their collective agenda. They were all eventually identified and exposed in the press, all the eager instruments of a strategy aimed at destabilizing fledgling democratic regimes and replacing them with docile plutocratic minions willing to underwrite America's politico-economic objectives while endorsing the Vatican's unfinished crusade.

What special bonds do Robert Macauley, J. Peter Grace and the Knights of Malta share? They all have close ties to the CIA and profess a strong penchant for ultra-right-wing causes. AmeriCares, whose declared mission is to offer relief worldwide *"regardless of race, religion or political persuasion,"* became active in Central America in the early 1980s, ferrying donations to U.S.-backed military regimes. It also contributed to and took sides in U.S.-engineered armed conflicts and routinely flew its armada into ideological battlefields directly linked to U.S. strategic interests.

Macauley had a long and intimate relationship with George Herbert Walker Bush -- they were childhood chums -- and he was a frequent guest at the U.S. intelligence apparatus Bush was to head as CIA director.

He was an enthusiastic supporter of the former president's deftly marketed *"Thousand Points of Light"* which, like all capitalistic solutions to severe socio-economic problems, did nothing to relieve misery in Central America and everything to further bolster the ruling pro-U.S. kleptocrats.

In 1985, disgraced Lt. Col. Oliver North got Unification Church head, the Rev. Sun Myung Moon, to fund $350,000 worth of supplies to the Contras. Three years earlier, the U.S. had withheld assistance to Sandinista Nicaragua, which had been devastated by a hurricane. It couldn't get its planes in fast enough when Violetta Chamorro, whose presidential campaign had been sponsored by the U.S. to the tune of $9 million, defeated the Sandinistas. On 28 February, 1990, barely three days after the election, AmeriCares' first shipment brought in 23 tons of medical supplies *"with love, from the people of the United States to the people of Nicaragua."* Nicaraguan diehard Cardinal Miguel Obando y Bravo took possession of the first shipment and turned it over to the well-connected Knights of Malta for distribution to a select list of recipients. President H. W. Bush's youngest son, Marvin, was aboard the next AmeriCares flight that landed days after Chamorro's inauguration. He was met by a Knights of Malta ambassador -- none other that Roberto Alejos Arzú, whose plantation had served as a CIA training ground for the 1961 Bay of Pigs fiasco, and a man known for his long association with some of Guatemala's most reactionary elements, including high-ranking clergy and military officers implicated in heinous human rights abuses.

Other prominent figures romped in this large incestuous bed: former CIA chief of counterintelligence, James Jesus Angleton; General (and later Secretary of State) Alexander Haig; former Nixon-Ford treasury secretary, William Simon; Reagan's envoy to the Vatican, William Wilson; and U.S. Senator Jeremiah Denton of Alabama, a "consultant" to Pat Robertson's Christian Broadcasting Network, who sponsored a bill allowing U.S. Air Force transports to ship goods for AmeriCares, a privilege accorded no other relief organization.

•

• •

Pope John Paul II first clashed with supporters of Liberation Theology during his 1983 visit to Central America. In Managua, he publicly humiliated the Rev. Ernesto Cardenal, a prominent human rights advocate whom he suspended from the priesthood. He paid a courtesy call on Salvadoran President Armando Calderon Sol, a member of the same political party that engineered activist Archbishop Romero's assassination and masterminded the massacre of 900 men, women and children at El Mozote. He then cavorted with barrel-chested colonels and generals, and granted audiences to high society women sporting low-cut dresses and dripping with diamonds -- instead of kneeling at the grave of six Jesuits slain by U.S.-trained death squads. The Pontiff then "retired" scores of vocal Latin American liberal clerics.

Hastened by papal nepotism strongly biased in favor

of diehard bishops, the purge of progressive clergy gained new momentum in Latin America. Tragically, in the most Catholic domain on earth, the "Golden Rule" was subverted by martial attitudes that view the faithful, at best as unruly sheep, at worst as the very enemies of the state. Astute and opportunistic, the Church tapped into the reactionary power base to maintain both doctrinal monopoly and political custody over the masses.

There is a precedent -- and a disquieting parallel. A thousand years ago, bloodhounds of orthodoxy sniffed heresy and the carnage began. People who held unacceptable views were flung into dungeons. Accused of harboring heterodox opinions, they were tortured with inventive cruelty, then killed. Often, before dying, they were forced to confess that they worshipped the devil *(translation: they toyed with free thought)*; indulged in hostile beliefs *(translation: they hungered for knowledge)*; and conspired against the established order *(translation: they spoke out against corruption and intellectual turpitude).*

This obscene quest, inspired and abetted by successive papal dynasties, was prelude to six "Crusades" during which hundreds of thousands of "infidels" -- Moslems and Jews -- were slaughtered. Religious fervor later fanned nearly four centuries of inquisitorial frenzy that devoured Europe and sent another half a million innocent people to the stake while their possessions, confiscated as "evidence," fattened the Church's coffers.

Like Karl Marx, who despised the proletariat, the Church has never fully expiated its disdain of the masses.

It steadfastly rejects the notion that people can govern their consciences without its guidance or control. Worse, it denies them the right to manage their political destinies by delivering them to the same reactionary Pharisaic elite that Jesus is said to have rebuked.

Few of Christianity's rulers, however pious, have lived up to the principles of Jesus, the radical who, if Biblical scribes did not tamper with the original script, is said to have preached compassion, pacifism and egalitarianism. Faced with a choice between Jesus' ethic and political expediency, Pope John Paul II sadly opted for the latter. He came to Latin America and told the poor that poverty ennobles the soul. He then pompously urged the rich Catholics who finance his reign to reject materialism. He might as well have ordered hyenas to abstain from eating meat. In casting out the good shepherds of Christianity from the fold, John Paul also surrendered the flock to the carnivores.

•

• •

It was the immorality of historical falsification -- and the baseness of academic dishonesty -- that propelled Montvert, a man with an unyielding respect for truth, on a lifelong campaign to unearth it wherever it may hide. He also transformed a passion for fine art into a medium through which he would later demonstrate that certain forms of human creativity cry out against lies, injustice and absurd beliefs.

His open mutiny against conformity began in high school.

His history teacher, Monsieur Delormel, routinely disregarded the obligatory French secular curriculum and shamelessly injected his personal prejudices and slanted perceptions. Armed with a razor-sharp intellect and a tongue to match, Delormel was a strict disciplinarian, a fount of erudition and a skilled pedagogue who would struggle, for two years, to educate Montvert or, as he had put it, "to deposit something of value inside this untidy, dissolute little brain of yours."

The broad knowledge Delormel possessed -- he was licensed to teach everything from algebra to zoology -- was often overshadowed by an appalling lack of objectivity. It was his very scholarship that enabled him, wherever he could, to skew history or to rewrite it by opining unabashedly about people long dead or editorializing about events exhaustively recorded in the otherwise unembellished lay French government curriculum.

A royalist, as are all devout French Catholics, Delormel steadfastly extenuated the arrogance and cruelty of French monarchs by insisting that they were, after all, "good Christians." It is true that kings and queens, when not making war, presiding over orgiastic banquets or fornicating with courtiers and servants alike, spent much time genuflecting in their private gilded chapels on ermine stoles and rich brocades while their vassals lived in squalor, starved and died of consumption. Distant abstractions, the horrors of the Crusades and the Inquisition elicited a kind of nostalgia from Delormel, if not a malicious admiration stripped of all misgivings for the atrocities committed in their name.

Montvert remembered learning about the events that took place on the night of August 23, 1572, better known as the Saint-Bartholomew massacre, during which 3,000 Huguenots were slaughtered in the streets of Paris on orders of her majesty, the unscrupulous but "Very Catholic" Queen of France, Catherine de Medici. News of the slaughter would be cheered by King Philip II, himself busy purging Spain of Protestants, Jews and Moors, and by Pope Gregory XIII who, for lack of more pressing business, reformed the calendar. Reviewing the incident did not seem to evoke in Montvert's teacher any discernible scruple.

Injecting personal bias into his instructions, Delormel presided over his own kangaroo court. He openly scorned the Huguenot Henri of Navarre, but lavished him with praise when, crowned Henri IV and fearful for his neck, he converted to Catholicism. *"Paris is well worth a mass,"* the king had sardonically remarked. Praise turned to condemnation when the king, now firmly enthroned, issued the Edict of Nantes, a decree restoring religious and political rights to French Protestants. A few chapters forward, the teacher applauded the edict's revocation, 87 years later, by the "Sun King," Louis XIV, the archetype warmongering despot whose conceit was eclipsed only by his lust for ostentation.

Fifty years hence, unaware of or utterly indifferent to the immense suffering his subjects endured, Louis XVI, who spent his reign tinkering with clocks, and his dizzy wife Marie-Antoinette, who plundered the nation's coffers to keep the court royally entertained, elicited pity and sympathy from Montvert's teacher.

"*They were very pious and joined in prayer several times a day.*"

As these enormities were being casually spouted, Montvert would retrieve from the depths of childhood memories Pathé and Fox newsreel footage of priests, their eyes turned to heaven sprinkling "holy water" on tanks and cannons and the fuselage of dive bombers so that Christians of one nation could wreak death and destruction upon Christians of another nation with the full blessings of Almighty God.

"A 'God' that takes sides," Montvert had snickered, "is on nobody's side." Delormel had removed him from class for the obligatory ten minute stroll up and down the hallway, a workout designed to "clear the brain."

The French Revolution, Monsieur Delormel insisted, was "*an outrage masterminded by Jewish financiers, Freemasons, degenerate philosophers and other irreligious libertines.*" This characterization, popular among Catholics, the titled and reactionaries, was nowhere to be found in the instruction manual Montvert had been issued -- nor in any history work he had since perused. He had found it amusing that, in reading assigned works by the chief "degenerate" French philosophers, Diderot, Montesquieu, Rousseau and Voltaire, he and his fellow students had been encouraged to parse and emulate their elegant literary style but enjoined from embracing their "amoral teachings."

"Imagine a student being told, 'Write like Hemingway but take care not to espouse his leftist values....' "Montvert was fond of saying.

The reign of terror that followed the fall of the Bastille on July 14, 1789 was summarily blasted as a *"grotesque act of barbarism against Christian values."* Yes, many innocent heads rolled during the two-year frenzy. But Monsieur Delormel could not bring himself to regard the insurrection as a cathartic spasm against centuries of misery and oppression or as the impetus that would help rid France, for the first time in history, of the yoke of feudalism, a dissolute clergy and a callous absolute monarchy.

The assassination, in his bathtub, of Jean-Paul Marat, a populist physician, lawyer, journalist and legislator in 1793, was flippantly dismissed as the *"extirpation of a Jewish scoundrel by a brave Catholic young woman* [Charlotte Corday]." Marat was not Jewish -- his parents were from Sardinia -- but Montvert's teacher had a quirky sense of humor that did not prevent him from creating myth where none existed.

Plant doubt among the uninformed and you can make them believe anything.

In contrast, the beheading of two royal idlers who bankrupted France while they wined, dined, gambled, gathered in prayer, made war and cheered their dogs on helpless foxes, Monsieur Delormel insisted, was murder. Nor would he entertain the notion that revolution, as Montvert perilously argued, is a process, not an incident. Many people tend to judge the French Revolution as a single event rather than a trend whose seeds were sown centuries earlier. The burgeoning concepts of human rights, equality, suffrage and the abolition of monarchy had actually taken root one hundred years before the storming of the Bastille.

Precocious, inquisitive and innately skeptical, Montvert survived and outgrew Monsieur Delormel's sinister brand of encoding. It wasn't until his own son came home one day from school crying, "the teacher said that Jews murdered Jesus," that he knew that chauvinism and encoding are alive and well, a new generation of freethinkers notwithstanding.

•

• •

A student of history and, if he can help it, a history maker, Father Hubert François de Ravaillac is a model Knight. When not discharging his apostolic duties or struggling with his conflicted sexuality with a daily auto-erotic regimen of self-whipping, he studies the newly updated secret Knights of Malta curriculum, *Recruitment and Training of an Auxiliary Army of God."* Filled with rapture at the thought that he is destined to play a unique role in God's magnificent scenario, he savors and commits to memory the following gems:

> ... The war for Christ is a territorial war. The "territory" is the human mind. The more completely captured in its raw state, the sooner it can be led to embrace our sacred doctrines and, in turn, programmed to help spread it. Once the mind has

been breached, the "political animal" is defeated; God triumphs and the Church can recapture the leadership and hegemony it once exercised in shaping the World in the Catholic tradition.

... In order to obtain optimal results, Christ's Soldiers must be among the most devout and obedient Catholics. They must be highly motivated. They must clearly understand the solemn nature and grave consequences of their obligation, and they must steadfastly justify their actions if unmasked or challenged. Sworn to secrecy, under no less a penalty than excommunication and spiritual death, they must be willing to suffer the vicissitudes and discomforts associated with our Holy Struggle, our war against infidels, and they must endure the animosity their mission will engender until we rise victorious.

... Well established citizens -- doctors, attorneys, business tycoons, teachers, journalists, and community leaders, all God-fearing, pious, church-going Catholics, shall be considered prime candidates for recruitment.

... When their participation in what inevitably will appear to be a covert operation is revealed to them they must be eager to proceed and infiltrate their social and professional circles.

... They will in turn receive instruction in techniques of persuasion and control of target individuals and groups. Awareness of and dedication to our noble struggle will be reinforced by --

Keeping the recruits highly motivated and inspired;

Encouraging the support of segments of society for an insurrection against heresy and for the overthrow and reconstruction of our current system of governance;

Impressing upon them that defeat will result in the adulteration and death of true Christianity, and in persecution;

Campaigning against avant-garde clergy, especially those who preach Liberation Theology, support the ordination of women to the priesthood, advocate the repeal of celibacy and endorse abortion, stem cell research and same-sex unions.

... Conscription will be carried out with due diligence in private consultations with recruiters who do not initially reveal their true identity. Recruits will then be informed that they are already inside the movement and that a change of heart is futile and carries severe penalties.

... Once trained, this legion of Christian soldiers will be charged with infiltrating unions, student groups, peasant organizations, school districts and regional legislative bodies.

In the name of the Father, the Son and the Holy Spirit, Amen.

If the verbiage gives off a strange odor of sulfur it's because it brazenly and tackily plagiarizes a clandestine and rather crude CIA training manual, *Psychological Operations in Counterinsurgency Warfare*, which was distributed in Nicaragua in the 80s by attaching clusters to balloons and floating them down into the countryside.

Drafted in Spanish, the 90-page manual advised U.S.-backed Contra rebels to *"kidnap and neutralize selected Nicaraguan government officials,"* a directive interpreted by Contra leaders to include assassination. It also suggested blackmailing Nicaraguan citizens into joining the rebel cause.

On February 5, 1984, the House Intelligence Committee concluded that production of the manual by the CIA violated a 1982 law that forbids U.S. personnel from taking part in the overthrow of the Nicaraguan government. Printed in Honduras, about 2,000 copies were distributed in 1983 to guerrillas of the Nicaraguan Democratic Force, the largest CIA-funded rebel force. Those attached to balloons were part of a 3,000-booklet edition cheaply printed at CIA headquarters in Langley, Virginia. Predictably, the House Intelligence Committee's ruling did not thwart future U.S. political, military and economic forays in Central America or, for that matter, elsewhere around the globe, all spearheaded by the CIA, which American author, Trevor Paglen, characterizes as

"an agency designed to operate outside the law ... free to pursue its vision of a new world, to create new geographies, and to keep that world's details far from the public record."

●

● ●

At odds with the modern world, Father Hubert believes that Catholic activists have too often struggled between their faith and the misguided or wavering convictions of the flock. Perhaps the enactment of a Catholic *sharia* (modeled after Islam's "divine" law) could greatly ease the Army of Christ's awesome task. Perhaps such sharia could also include a *fatwa*, or decree, that sanctions, in the name of the Lord, the formation of death squads charged with the ritual execution of heretics and apostates. Spurning the lessons of history, trembling with sacramental fervor, Hubert François de Ravaillac, the descendant of Huguenot King Henry IV's assassin will be ready if called. After all, he was named in honor of Saint Hubert, the patron saint of hunters.

LETTER FROM ROTTERDAM

L ATE ON THE AFTERNOON of October 2, 2008, the phone chimes in the cluttered riverfront office of Michel Montvert, director of the Institute of Symbolic and Hermetic Arts in Paris. On the line is Dr. Manuel Albeniz, a colleague and specialist in Medieval history in Madrid.

"I received a letter this morning from a certain Jan van den Haag. Did you?" Albeniz asks in heavily accented French.

"I don't know. Why."

"His signature is followed by a CC addressed to you."

"Let me look."

Montvert, a tall, angular, graying man, leans across his desk. The in-box brims with sheaves of documents and unopened mail. He finds the envelope. Peering at the tight, florid script in which his name and address are inscribed, he turns around, leans back in his high-winged leather chair and stretches his feet on the credenza. Through the window, across the slate-colored Seine, the filigreed spires of the Sainte-Chapelle shimmer in the pale pastel colors of dusk. Frozen in time, stupor or lethargy or anguish etched on their granite faces, winged and serpent-like, their shadows stretching over the battlements, gargoyles fix vacant but ever-watchful eyes on the city below.

"I found it."

"Will you have a chance to read it soon?"

"I doubt it. I've been swamped. I'm exhausted. Yesterday I gave a lecture on Frida Kahlo at the Musée d'Orsay. This morning we had a retrospective of the late Jules Perahim's work. The Bauhaus Museum in Berlin has invited me to address a symposium. I'm flying out tonight. I'll try to read it on the plane."

"Do that," Albeniz presses with some urgency. "You'll find it ... intriguing. Let me hear from you when you get back."

"*De acuerdo. Hasta pronto, hermano.*" Deep in thought, Montvert lets out a wearied sigh, fans himself distractedly with the envelope, and stows it in his breast pocket.

●

● ●

In his office at the El Prado Museum, Albeniz, an older man with a high forehead and a lion-like mane of silvery hair, rereads the missive. He frowns, and shakes his head. Grimace turns to grin, grin to sneer.

"*Nah, debe ser una broma.*" Must be a joke. There's more hope than certitude in this assessment. Something in Jan van den Haag's language, in the elegance of his syntax, in his carefully articulated esotericism and allusions reveals broad scholarship and implies initiation into and familiarity with the symbolism and objectives of Freemasonry. His entreaty has the resonance of truth.

Most enticing are the data he promises to share in future communications, should Albeniz and Montvert express serious interest.

That evening, as the Airbus that carries Montvert to Berlin descends toward Tempelhof Airport, Albeniz heads to La Escudilla Restaurant, in the Barrio de Trafalgar, for a late supper. He eats absent-mindedly struggling to reconcile history, art, human nature and the politics of discretion.

•
• •

In his room at the venerable Hotel de Rome on Bebelplatz, off the lime-tree-lined Unter den Linden in the German capital, Montvert reviews his notes for the next day's symposium. He remembers van den Haag's letter, still resting in the breast pocket of his jacket. He walks to the closet, retrieves it and stretches on the king-sized bed. Once again, he studies the exquisite penmanship, the stamp, the postmark. He wearily tears the envelope open and removes a sheet of buff-hued paper bearing an impeccably symmetrical italic hand-written message.

P.O.B 3579, Rotterdam, The Netherlands
30 September 2008
Dear Monsieur Montvert,

We share similar interests, political leanings and metaphysical ideals, many of them embodied in the Regius Poem and later reaffirmed in Anderson's

Constitution. You and I are also heir to the same wanderings and tribulations that have darkened the pages of history. It is in that spirit that I write.

I am the direct and last descendant of a legendary artist whose name I cannot reveal at this time. In my possession is a manuscript this early freethinker penned shortly before he died. A codicil stipulates that it will not be opened and circulated until five hundred years after his death. The document has been safeguarded by my family over the centuries and his injunction was scrupulously respected -- until now. Old, unmarried and childless, unsure I will reach the year 2016, when the contents of my ancestor's revelations can be made public, guilt-ridden but consumed with curiosity, I broke the wax seal and perused an extraordinary compendium of insights and affirmations about his work, personal convictions and the perils of whimsy -- or grotesque realism -- in an age of austere literalism. What I read has left me shaken, enthralled, confused and apprehensive.

Your reputation and that of Señor Albeniz in the world of art and art history are unrivaled. So is your untiring patronage of Surrealism, primitive and contemporary, as are Señor Albeniz's grasp of inter-doctrinal affairs and expertise on the rift that continues to divide the Church and the secular world.

My forebear's musings, I believe, need to be made public, studied and deliberated. The airing of this startling document can only be entrusted to a professional, someone whose character, eminence and authority command attention, someone who can stand firm against the firestorm of controversy, perhaps of rancor, that my ancestor's final words are apt to ignite.

If you wish to learn more and, having done so, can pledge your willingness to shepherd what will surely result in a scandal of sizable magnitude, please write. If not, I apologize for the intrusion with every assurance that I shall bear you not a trace of ill will.

Respectfully and Fraternally,
Jan Henryk van den Haag.
CC. Dr. Manuel Albeniz

Van den Haag's ornate signature ends with three dots forming an equilateral triangle.

In his luxurious quarters at the papal apartments, Pope Benedict XVI consults with the second most powerful man in the Catholic Church hierarchy, his successor and trusted Inquisitor, the hard-nosed Cardinal William Joseph Levada. The *in-camera* tête-à-tête focuses on two matters. The first concerns a projected trip by the pontiff to the Middle East, where he will try to mend fences with Jews and Muslims. The second explores new strategies aimed at hardening the Church's stance on Freemasonry, more specifically the official branding of Catholics who join Masonic lodges as heretics guilty of a mortal sin.

As prefect of the Congregation for the Doctirne of the Faith, then pope-in-training, Joseph Cardinal Ratzinger earned a reputation as a hard-line enforcer of Catholic doctrinal absolutism. After heaping syrupy praise on René Descartes, the 17th century French rationalist philosopher, Ratzinger abruptly suspended his homage by condemning Descartes and forbidding Catholics to read his books "on pain of sin." He condemned Liberation Theology, the oxygen-rich ministry that redefines and, for the poor and voiceless, enlivens an otherwise stolid Roman Catholicism, and he punished its disciples with public humiliations, swift and irrevocable defrocking, and summary excommunications. He also excoriated and suppressed neo-liberal theologians and delivered hostile orations against abortion, homosexuality and the ordination of women to the priesthood.

When Benedict ascended to the Papacy his election was halfheartedly welcomed by some Jewish groups (one of them the right-wing and very accommodating Anti-Defamation League, which is more interested in ingratiating itself with the Vatican than in rehashing history). He received a more tepid welcome from world Jewry which hoped that Benedict would *"continue along the path of Pope John XXIII and Pope John Paul II in supporting the State of Israel and committing to an uncompromising fight against anti-Semitism."*

Critics accuse Benedict's papacy of being insensitive towards Judaism. They cite the expanding use of the Tridentine Mass, which calls for the conversion of Jews to Christianity, and denounce the reinstatement of four excommunicated bishops, all members of the Society of

St. Pius X, a traditionalist and virulently anti-Semitic Catholic organization. One of these bishops is American Richard Williamson, an outspoken Holocaust denier who struggled to issue a skewed apology but did not recant his position on the well documented event.

Pope Benedict's dealings with Islam -- 1.2 billion-strong and growing at about three percent per year -- remain, at best, strained. On September 12, 2006 the pontiff delivered a lecture at the University of Regensburg in Germany, where he had served as professor of theology. Entitled *"Faith, Reason and the University -- Memories and Reflections,"* the lecture received critical attention from political and religious authorities. Muslim politicians and religious leaders recoiled at his pompous insensitivity and protested against what they perceived to be inflammatory rhetoric and an odious mischaracterization of Islam. They were especially offended by the following statement:

> "Show me just what Muhammad brought that was new and there you will find things only evil and inhuman, such as his command to spread by the sword the faith he preached."

The pope said nothing about the Crusades, the "Holy" Inquisition and the "Conquest" of the Americas, which, in addition to fattening the Church's bulging treasury, were waged to spread Christianity … by the sword.

Other pontifical gaffes would follow, all dramatic evidence of a Church woefully out of touch with reality, to say nothing of how prone it is to tinker with history.

On his first visit overseas, Benedict told a gathering of Latin American bishops in Brazil that preaching Jesus and his gospel did not intrude upon or corrupt pre-Columbian cultures. This callous falsehood triggered a storm of indignation, prompting the Vatican to issue a hasty but unconvincing "clarification," not a *Mea Culpa*. Instead of expressing regret for the evils of colonialism and forced conversions, the clarification indemnified the modern Church by disingenuously claiming that it in no way condones the excesses of the past.

When Benedict was elected pope, one of his first and perhaps most surprising supporters was PETA (People for the Ethical Treatment of Animals). PETA expediently or naïvely portrays Jesus as a vegetarian, which he may have been when he was not eating fish, but in whose honor the ritual of Holy Communion turns his followers into cannibals. The pontiff's passion for traditional papal garb, especially gold-embroidered ermine-trimmed vestments, once a royal entitlement, prompted animal lovers everywhere to ask Benedict to live up to his words and give fur a rest. No one knows for sure whether such mundane petition had any effect on papal prerogative.

Distancing himself yet again from actuality, bent on taking the Church back to its darkest days, Benedict, on his first trip to Africa, a continent where at least 25 million people are infected with HIV, told the gathered masses that condoms are not only useless in the prevention of AIDS but that they may actually aggravate the problem. The "cruel epidemic," he insisted, should be tackled through "fidelity and abstention." Reckless faith, or depraved cynicism still prevents the pope from grasping the enormity of his counsel. Pro-life -- the protoplasmic kind -- but indifferent to the dignity of man, his outrageous directive condemns millions to an early, agonizing death.

•

• •

Tired, facing a busy schedule, Montvert surrenders to fitful, dream-haunted sleep. In the morning he will be speaking about the great Kandinsky, one of the most important innovators in modern art. The painter's abstract, obsessively geometric, brightly colored canvases of incredible sensorial richness coalesce and break apart in a kaleidoscope of Montvert's own nightmare-induced creation. Further along in the dream, he enters the Bauhaus, the legendary German art and architecture school from which so many modernists would emerge. Suddenly, the edifice crumbles around him, as it did figuratively in 1933 when the Nazis, fearing the "un-German" (Jewish) influence of social liberals and the impact of "degenerate art" on the pristine Teutonic psyche, shut its doors for the remainder of the war.

This is no longer Joseph Goebbels' domain but Montvert has yet to feel at ease in Germany. His discomfort is visceral. Germans may have collectively expiated the sins of their fathers but there is something about their country that he finds troubling -- the language, clipped, guttural, brusque, imperious -- the frosty aloofness, the uniforms, the mannerisms, the formalistic infatuation with "discipline" and "order," the reemergence of Nazi cells, the transparent nostalgia for the Third Reich's brief but intoxicating rapture. All hark back to a time, not so very long ago, when Germans enthusiastically goose-stepped to Hitler's drumbeat. Even in his sleep, Montvert can't wait to clear off.

•

• •

Albeniz, an insomniac, walks home as Madrid's other self, iridescent and roguish, comes to life in the late evening hours. Lost in thought, brooding over Jan van den Haag's baffling letter, he turns to another time when darkness reigned, when blindness to man's inhumanity and deafness to reason were self-inflicted attitudes, not congenital infirmities. Somewhere in the distance church bells strike eleven.

"We have learned nothing," he says to himself as he unlocks his apartment door and retires for the night.

•

• •

Night in the Middle Ages is neither longer nor shorter than it's ever been but it's infinitely darker, filled with impenetrable shadows, and few venture into the sulfurous chasm for there, under a thick mantle of ignorance, superstition and aberrant beliefs, dwell in untold numbers the loathsome incarnations of man's most hideous fears. Fear of the unknown. Fear of change. Fear of observable truth. Fear of witches, demons, ravenous incubi and insatiable succubi. Fear of temptation. Fear of God's pitiless tribunal. Fear of Hades and Satan. Fear of sin and eternal damnation.

As day slowly blanches away the blackness, only the sky dares to brighten. The monstrous visions that populate night retreat for a while but they do not vanish. They return at a time of their own choosing. Day scatters the gloom but it sheds no light. It's just an optical illusion, a hesitant and fleeting sensation on the retina, not a higher state of consciousness or wisdom. It is in the full blaze of sunlight that the real horror resumes, this time inflicted upon the flesh, not dreamed; branded on the soul, not imagined. The nightmare is real, fed by a collective hallucination that will bloody the pages of history for the next four hundred years.

In 1314, charged with heresy, Jacques de Molay, the last Grand Master of the Knights Templar is burned at the stake on orders of Pope Clement V, King Philip IV's all-too-obliging yes-man.

"Damned," "accursed," "banned," are Spanish epithets reserved for Marranos, the crypto-Jews of the Iberian Peninsula who, by coercion or out of pragmatism, convert to Christianity in the aftermath of the pogroms of 1391. These *"conversos,"* as they are also called, number more than 100,000. With them the history of the Jews enters a new phase. Hatred of the Jews sparks the introduction of the Inquisition in Spain and hastens their mass expulsion from the Iberian Peninsula.

The Marranos and their descendants are divided into three groups. Some are indifferent to Judaism or any other religion; they welcome the opportunity to trade oppression for the lucrative careers and life of ease opened to them as Christians. The phenomenon inspires the bitter quip, *"Conversion is an ignominy of which only Jews are capable...."* Others cherish the Jewish faith, preserve traditions and secretly attend synagogue. Others yet, by far the largest in numbers, yield to circumstances, posture as Catholics but remain Jews in their home life and religious rituals.

Incited by the Catholic clergy, Marranos, many among them cultured and affluent, arouse the envy and hatred of the populace. They are routinely hounded and mistreated. The first in a series of riots against them breaks out in Toledo in 1449 and is accompanied by murder and pillage. Prompted by two priests, the mob plunders and burns scores of homes. Another attack takes place in Toledo in July 1467. Some 1,600 houses are consumed. Many Marranos perish in the flames or are slain, some by hanging.

Six years later, emulating Toledo, Córdoba erupts in a conflict pitting Christians and Marranos. On March 14, 1473, during a religious procession, a young girl inadvertently spills the contents of a chamber pot from her window, splashing an image of the Virgin Mary. Outraged, thousands join in a strident call for revenge. The mob pounces on the Marranos, accusing them of heresy, killing them and burning their houses. Girls are raped. Men, women, and children are put through the sword. The massacre and pillage lasts three days and nights. To prevent the repetition of such excesses, Marranos are expelled from Córdoba.

Attacks on Marranos spread to other cities, where they are killed, their houses ransacked and their possessions purloined.

The advent of the Inquisition is followed by an edict forcing Jews to retreat to their ghettoes. Issued by King Ferdinand and Queen Isabella "the Catholic," the edict lays the groundwork for the deportation and exile of the Jews from the country. The decree of expulsion materially increases the number, already large, of those who purchase freedom in their beloved homeland by accepting baptism.

More obsessive than the Spaniards', the hatred of the Portuguese toward the Jews, which had long smoldered, turns to violence in Lisbon. On April 17, 1506, a Dominican priest rouses the populace and, crucifix in hand, strolls through the streets of the city, crying "Heresy!" and calling upon the people to exterminate the Marranos. More than 500 Marranos are massacred and incinerated on the first day. The innocent victims of popular fury, young and old, living and dead, are dragged from their houses and thrown pell-mell upon the pyre. By the second day, at least 2,000 Marranos perish.

In 1562, foreshadowing *Kristallnacht* and the ensuing genocide nearly four centuries later, and to facilitate the planned slaughter of more Marranos, high-ranking Church officials decree that they be required to wear special badges and confined to the ghettoes. The yellow star patch and crude tattoos would come later.

Under constant threat of persecution, destitution and death, the Marranos take flight. Many emigrate. Some go to Italy. Others settle in France, Flanders and The Netherlands. Others yet flee as far east as Greece, Romania, Bulgaria, Turkey and the Levant.

Large numbers of Marranos, however, stay put. Many in Madrid, conscious of their Jewish heritage, are well disposed toward the Jews. Some, like Manuel Albeniz, patronize La Escudilla, a popular kosher restaurant.

●

●   ●

Accused by the church of being a relapsed heretic at a farcical trial engineered to placate the English Court, Joan of Arc is burned at the stake in 1431. Her ashes are dumped in the Seine. A retrial 25 years later establishes her innocence and she is declared a martyr. It will take nearly 500 years before she is "beatified," a status that entitles the faithful to seek the intervention of a dead person in their private affairs. Eleven years later she is canonized a saint and granted a permanent seat in heaven.

In 1468 the Flemish city of Ghent is sacked and the first documented Church-mandated tortures and executions take place, "to fight the Devil's work."

Alain de la Roche, a French Dominican priest, writes and illustrates an "authoritative" treatise on the creatures, some real, others skillfully improvised, that personify "sin." The demented tract is promptly endorsed by the Church and circulated among high-ranking prelates.

In 1481, the "Holy" Inquisition, under the bestial

tutelage of Tomas de Torquemada -- himself the grandson of a *"converso"* -- and acting on behalf of the king and queen, engages in wholesale persecution, torture, murder and expropriations masterminded to purge Spain of the Jews and to enrich the Church.

Six years later, backed by a papal bull (edict) the German inquisitor Heinrich Kramer publishes the *Malleus Maleficarum*, or Witches' Hammer, a manual that "ascertains the existence" of witchcraft. Challenging and chastising skeptics, the *Malleus* offers "evidence" that witches are more often women than men. It trains inquisitors to identify them, describes the physical characteristics of the "possessed" and teaches their tormentors the essential methods (think *"enhanced interrogation techniques,"* -- including water-boarding) most effective against a long list of imaginary trans-gressions. A latter-day variation on the theme, *phrenology,* a thoroughly discredited late 18th century pseudoscience based on the false assumption that mental faculties (or the lack thereof) can be identified by palpation of the skull, would unfairly brand certain people morons, criminals and perverts -- labels that better describe the practitioners of this quackery than their unwitting subjects.

Repression escalates and spreads like wildfire.

Jews are expelled from Spain. In Portugal they are forced to convert to Christianity -- or else. So are the Moors. The persecution continues under the reign of King Philip II and Pope Clement VIII. Openly anti-Semitic, the pontiff links Jews with usury -- the only occupation they are legally entitled to pursue, not with their own money but with funds supplied to them and controlled by an elite of rich, non-Jewish trades people.

Barely concluded, the One Hundred Year War stokes the political and religious discord that cleaves France and England. It will take nearly four centuries for the enmity to cease.

The plague, cholera and a host of venereal diseases erupt, claiming thousands in their wake. The Jews are blamed for spreading these scourges.

Religious frictions, awakened by isolated efforts to breathe fresh air into the Church and resisted by those who aspire to dogmatize it further, threaten to destroy the very fabric of Christianity

Members of a Calvinist sect in Northern Italy are nearly exterminated by the Armies of French king Francis I in a campaign billed as a "crusade against religious perversion."

In 1497, Girolamo Savonarola, book-burner and self-styled moralizer and prior of St. Mark's convent in Italy, is excommunicated by Pope Alexander VI. A year later he is roasted alive in the public square where the Bonfire of the Vanities had once blazed. His crime: he preaches against narcicism and the unbridled moral turpitude of the clergy.

Charged with heresy -- endorsing and promoting the Copernican theory that the Sun, not the Earth is the center of our solar system -- Italian philosopher and pantheist Giordano Bruno is expelled from the Dominican Order in 1576. He aggravates his case by arguing that the physical universe is infinite and asserting that human beings are not unique because the presence of life, even that of rational beings, may not be confined to planet Earth. He signs his death warrant when he affirms that absolute knowledge is a myth and that there are no limits to the advancement of learning. He is burned alive. [In 2000, on the quadricentennial commemoration of his execution, the Vatican issues a statement, troubling in its ambiguity and cynicism, insisting that Bruno's death was *"a sad episode of Christian history"* but that his writings were *"incompatible with Christian thinking and he remains a heretic."*]

Luther, the firebrand reformer, drives a wedge that irreparably widens the abyss dividing Christians and alters the course of western civilization. His ferocious anti-Semitism, his venomous tracts provide the template for the modern hatred of the Jews. His last vituperations, three days before his death, call for the expulsion of all Jews from Germany.

Heresy is defined as opinion or doctrine that sharply contrasts with orthodox religious principles or, as historian David Christie-Murray observes,

> "an opinion held by a minority of men which the majority declares is unacceptable and, therefore, strong enough to punish."

Contemporary forms of deviation from "declared" majority opinion are variously called "treason," "subversion," "civil disobedience," and "sedition."

In a world dominated by darkness, not everyone wants to see the light. Still, it is the very nature of light, however feeble or tentative, to seek an aperture through which it can escape. And even during these murky, cruel times when blind faith smothers sanity and obscures reason, faint streams of clarity emerge and signal a tardy rebirth, a slow and hesitating cleansing from the madness.

Alive in the uncommon man is the urge and promise of self-knowledge and an intuitive commitment to the rational exploration of the universe around him. This is no easy task, in any epoch, least of all in the Middle Ages when unsupported opinions and unchallenged convictions overshadow knowledge, when ideological rigidity stifles inquiry and the psyche is forever held prisoner by monsters of its own making. It is the desire to free the soul from its shackles and to elevate it to higher spheres of intellect that arms the nascent freethinker with the courage to probe beyond the limits of mass myopia. While new ideas are heresy to the blinkered, they are glimpses of exhilarating and perilous truth to the enlightened who spurn religious authority, resist the tyranny of forced ideas, favor scientific scrutiny and advocate rational discourse. Such profanation of canon law is swiftly and harshly frustrated by the Church. From Saint Peter to recent history, and while proclaiming its God-given authority over mere mortals, the papacy exhibits a propensity for corruption, deceit, murder, torture, rape, pedophilia, incest and prostitution that diverts attention from and weakens the early triumphs of tolerance, individualism and non-conformity.

•

• •

It all begins, like many conquests, with a single proclamation by a self--promoting egomaniac leveled at simple-minded, humble peons craving for a better morrow.

"As he was going along by the Sea of Galilee, He saw Simon Peter and Andrew, the brother of Simon, casting a net in the sea, for they were fishermen.
"And Jesus said to them, "Follow me and I will make you become fishers of men."
"And they immediately abandoned their nets and followed Him."

Peter is hailed as the first of twelve disciples. And thus, near the Mediterranean port of Caesarea, according to Matthew's narrative, written 90 years after the death of Jesus, and Mark's anonymous and paradoxical account of events, are uttered the words that launched the Church, made Simon (called Peter) the first pope and kindled the early fires of anti-Semitism.

The first thirteen popes bridge a period that extends to the year 190 of the Christian Era. In other words, an average of 4.4 men per year are elevated to the Church's highest rung during that time. The turnover rate is four times higher than that of the busiest whorehouse in Rome. From the beginning, popes establish criteria for admittance to Christianity. These norms, which, in defiance of Jesus' universalist teachings, exclude "apostates," and other "undesirables," are quickly politicized and incorporated by force into the civil codes of the ruling lay elite. In effect, the state has the power, which it uses without scruple, to prosecute and punish what the Church considers crimes against the state ... and Christianity.

From the beginning, the clergy and the Catholicized nobility commit horrific acts of violence. A papal election is always preceded or followed by fist-fights and worse. Careerists and upstarts clash with fanatics and fundamentalists. What follows are the extravagances, entrenched mediocrity, inertia and sleaze, the criminal neutrality and eager connivances, the decadence and the scandals that would sully the Church and give religion the bad name it continues to earn.

POPES, PIMPS, PROSTITUTES

POPE NICHOLAS V issues a papal bull granting the King of Portugal the right to reduce *"Saracens, pagans and other unbelievers"* to hereditary slavery, and to kill them if they resist.

Urban II grants "remission of all their sins" to those undertaking "a military enterprise" designed "to liberate eastern churches [those established in the 'Holy Land'] from heretics" -- the Jews and Muslims.

Callixtus III bans all interaction between Christians and Jews not designed to dispossess the Jews.

Aloof, inaccessible, given to fits of weeping, utterly inept in statecraft, lacking distinction and achieving nothing of consequence for Italy or Christendom, Paul II delights at the sight of naked men being racked and tortured and displays an extravagant love of personal splendor that gratifies his overblown sense of self-worth.

Sixtus IV, a champion of the Spanish Inquisition, sires six illegitimate sons, one the fruit of an incestuous affair with his own sister.

Innocent VIII instigates severe measures against *"magicians and witches."* He confirms Torquemada as Grand Inquisitor of Spain. His reign will be known as the Golden Age of Bastards.

Julius II obtains the pontificate by fraud and bribery.

Pius II writes erotic novels. He showers praise on the Prince of Walachia, the notorious Vlad the Impaler (Dracula) who shish-kebabs his enemies and fickle friends alike. The pope fathers about twelve illegitimate children.

Leo X is a shopaholic. He finances his spending sprees by selling indulgences, a racket that grants, for a fee, full or partial remission of temporal punishment for sins already forgiven. Under his pontificate, Christianity assumes a pagan character.

Alexander VI, the notorious Mr. Borgia, is without a doubt the most evil and corrupt pope in history. He becomes a byword for the depraved standards of the papacy. He finagles his way to St. Peter's by making cardinals out of crooked cronies so they could vote for him. He also appoints his son, Cesare, and the teenage brother of his mistress cardinals. Being the "Holy Father" does not prevent Mr. Borgia from engaging in an active sex life, engineering the murder of his rivals, indulging in orgies and siring seven children. To help "build alliances," he forces his daughter Lucrezia into three miserable unions. Her fourth marriage, to a man she does not dislike, ends in tragedy when the alliance goes sour and the pontiff orders him stabbed to death. Mr. Borgia encourages the slave trade in "conquered" lands in the "Indies," to facilitate conversions to Christianity. He dies of syphilis.

Paul III creates the Congregation of the Holy Office of the Inquisition. His rationale:

"Punishment does not take place primarily and

per se for the correction and good of the person punished, but for the public good in order that others may become terrified and weaned away from the evils they would commit."

The thought police is born. In 1908, the name of the agency is changed to The Sacred Congregation of the Holy Office. It is again rechristened in 1965 as The Congregation for the Doctrine of the Faith. Cardinal Joseph Alois Ratzinger, now Pope Benedict XVI, serves as Prefect of that all-powerful body, whose chief mission is to safeguard and promote Catholic doctrine, faith and ethics throughout the world. The new Inquisition professes a similar objective. It is a permanent institution of the Catholic Church. It justifies or casts a blind eye on unspeakable crimes in its frenetic crusade against heresy. Led by a Byzantine central bureaucracy, the Vatican responds to any deviation from its edicts with swift and wrathful retribution. Adding cynicism to unspeakable obtuseness, it continues to preach that political necessity is at the root of the Inquisition, past and present.

No doubt aroused by their sensuality, Pope Paul IV orders exquisite nudes painted by Michelangelo on the ceiling of the Sistine Chapel to be covered up.

Pope Innocent X, in yet another campaign of prudery, has a charming newborn Jesus painted by Guercino wrapped with a shirt.

Leonardo da Vinci is driven underground. Cervantes is placed on the Index of forbidden authors. So are Bacon, Maimonides, Petrarch and Rabelais. Tax-exempt and immune from honest labor, fat and opulent, the Church and the aristocracy harass and exploit the serfdom. In their shadow, rich merchants fleece their patrons and bleed the populace.

Across the Atlantic, the plunder of the Americas by bearded savages brandishing a sword in one hand and wielding a cross in the other is in full swing, punctuated by forced conversions, looting, rape and genocide.

●

● ●

Most Christians never hear a disparaging word about popes, some of whom have risen to mythical status. It's as if a perpetual halo of saintliness hovers over their heads. Yet the history of the papacy bears no resemblance to its modern-day portrayal. Over time, the truth about them has been obscured. Their true character was so craftily altered, or glossed over, that few people realize that scores of popes were not only decadent but were also the most savage warring men ever known. Egomaniacal, lustful self-promoters who wallowed in vice -- traits Catholic historians conceal -- popes were widely resented and feared by the laity. When the early glow of Enlightenment awakened heretofore blinkered minds, freethinkers rebelled against them. Doctrinal disobedience steeled the papacy and led to new pinnacles of barbarism.

With the unctuous gentility of modern papacy as a backdrop, it is hard to imagine that the ancient gurus of Christendom were brutal thugs who retaliated against "heresy" with torture and death. Popes waded through torrents of blood to fulfill their earthly objectives and many led their mercenaries on evangelical fields of battle from which they returned enriched through murder and pillage.

Bishop Liutprand of Cremona, author of the *Antapodosis*, a florid but highly literate satire of the kings of the first half of the 10th century, paints a remarkable portrait of the debauchery of the popes and their sacerdotal confederates, perhaps with a tinge of envy:

> "They hunted on horses with gold trappings, feasted at rich banquets with dancing girls when the hunt was over, and retired with these shameless whores to beds lined with silk sheets and gold-embroidered covers. All the Roman bishops were married, and their wives made silk dresses out of the sacred vestments."

Christian historians dismiss with annoying flippancy the true character of the popes, arguing that they never considered them "faultless." Yet they keep on whitewashing their evil doings. It is in the nature of proselytism, political or religious, to *mis*-inform when it can, to *dis*-inform when it must. The truth drowns in the process.

Pope John XII, one in a long dynasty of dissolute popes, put his mistress Marcia, a prostitute, in charge of his brothel in the Lateran Palace. He *"liked to have around him a collection of Scarlet Women,"* wrote Benedict of Soracte, a 10th century monk-historian the Catholic Encyclopedia smugly dismisses. At the pope's trial for the murder of a rival, his clergy swore that he had engaged in incest with his sisters and had raped his nuns. He and his mistresses got so soused at a banquet that they accidentally set fire to the building. In an epoch when the average tenure of a pope was less than two years, John XII sat on St. Peter's throne for a decade. His life came to a sudden and violent end when, according to Church officials, he was slain by the Devil while raping a woman. The truth is prosaic and infinitely more gratifying. The Holy Father was beaten so severely by the woman's husband that he died of his injuries a week later.

On occasion, the Catholic Encyclopedia provides grudging accounts of papal misconduct. The scandal surrounding Pope Benedict IX is a case in point. In 1032, after clawing his way up to the papacy, he promptly excommunicates clerics he considers hostile and launches a reign of terror. He opens the doors of the papal palace to homosexuals and turns it into a lucrative male brothel. His violent and licentious conduct infuriates the citizens of Rome who replace him with John of Sabine, crowned Pope Sylvester III. But Sylvester is driven out by Benedict's brothers. Benedict sells the papacy to his godfather, Giovanni Graziano, later known as Pope Gregory VI. Benedict then engineers a coup and reclaims the papal seat. The Church grudgingly remembers him as

"… immoral, cruel and indifferent to spiritual things … depraved and unsuited for the ascetic life. He was the worst pope since John XII."

Upon Benedict's death, undertakers refuse to build him a coffin. He is hastily interred in a shroud under the cover of darkness.

According to the testimony of St. Bruno, the learned, self-effacing and frugal founder of the Carthusian Order of cloistered contemplative monks,

> "The whole Church was in wickedness, holiness had faded, justice had perished, and truth had been buried ... popes and bishops were given to luxury and fornication. The training of the popes left much to be desired, the moral standard of many being very low and the practice of celibacy seldom observed. Bishops obtained their offices in irregular ways; their lives and conversations were strangely at variance with their calling. They discharged their duties, not for Christ but for motives of worldly gain. The clergy were in many places regarded with scorn, and their avaricious ideas, opulence and immorality rapidly gained ground at the center of clerical life. When ecclesiastical authority grew weak at the fountainhead, it necessarily decayed elsewhere. Papal authority lost the respect of many, inspiring resentment against the Curia [the body of tribunals and offices through which the pope governs the Catholic Church] and against the papacy."

Showing contempt for titles, Bruno declined to be made bishop, withdrew with a group of followers and built a monastery.

Pope Leo IX was an unscrupulous buccaneer who

spent his pontificate sightseeing Europe with a retinue of armed knights and left the world worse than he had found it. The Church calls him "lapsed," coyly admitting that

> "He defected from the faith... he fell away by actually offering sacrifice to the false gods."

St. Peter Damian (1007-1072), an aficionado of self-mortification, and the fiercest censor of his age, unrolled a frightful picture of decay in clerical morality in the lurid pages of his *Book of Gomorrah*, a curious document that remarkably survived centuries of Church cover-ups and book-burnings. He wrote:

> "A natural tendency to murder and brutalize appears with the popes. Nor do they have any inclination to conquer their abominable lust; many are seen to have employed into licentiousness for an occasion to the flesh, and hence, using this liberty of theirs, perpetuating every crime."

British historian Lord Acton (1834-1902) summed up the martial nature of the popes when he noted,

> "They not only murdered in the great style, but they also made murder a legal basis of the Christian Church and a condition of salvation."

Perhaps the popes were dutifully obeying Jesus' command:

"But those mine enemies which would not that I reign over them, bring hither and slay before me." (Luke, 19:27).

Today's Christian clergy works diligently to represent Jesus as an inspired but harmless preacher and a prophet of peace. But they cagily avoid any discussion of the passage from the Gospels that nullifies in one sentence everything Christianity purports to embody. Are proponents of the death penalty and the lunatics who advocate the murder of abortion doctors merely human, or do they knowingly draw their inspiration from that ruthless telltale verse?

•

• •

The "magnificent 12th century" that the faithful inexplicably glorify above all others of the Dark Ages, begins with the Inquisition, which lingers in various forms for the next six centuries, and ushers in the 35-year crusade against the Cathars (also known as the Albigenses). The Catholic Encyclopedia readily acknowledges -- and obliquely rationalizes -- the Church's arrogance and tyrannical nature when it describes the Inquisition as

"a special ecclesiastical institution for combating or suppressing heresy -- 'heresy' meaning 'holding a different opinion'."

Establishment of the Inquisition was the only time in Christian history when the Church was united in purpose and spoke with one voice. The Inquisition became a permanent office of Christianity and, to justify its principles and objectives, the popes introduced a persuasive instrument in the form of fictitious documents known as *The Forged Decretum of Gratian*. The forgeries constitute some of the greatest impostures known to mankind, the most successful and most stubborn in their hold on unenlightened people. Philosopher John William Draper calls them

> "a mass of fabrications ... that made the whole Christian world, through the papacy, the domain of the Italian clergy. It inculcated that it is lawful to constrain men to goodness, to torture and execute heretics and to confiscate their property; that to kill an excommunicated person is not murder, that the pope, in his unlimited superiority to all law, stands on an equality with the Son of God."

The darker features of that era are not in dispute among honest historians. In this period of Christian history, hundreds of thousands of people were massacred by the Church. In 1182, Pope Lucius III grabbed control of the Church and two years later declared the Cathars heretics and authorized a crusade against them. A crusade is a gratuitous war instigated by the Church for alleged religious ends, and sanctioned by a papal bull.

Eighty-six years earlier, in 1096, Pope Urban II approved the first of eight crusades -- there would be a total of nineteen -- and they went on for 475 years. Heresy, the Church declared, was a blow in the face of God and it was the duty of every Christian to kill heretics. Earlier still, Pope Gregory VII officially asserted that *"the killing of heretics is not murder,"* and decreed it legal for the Church to slay "non-believers." Up until the 19th century, popes forced Christian monarchs to make heresy a crime punishable by death under their civil codes. But it was not heresy that inspired the crusade against the Cathars. Its purpose was to give the papacy additional land and revenues. The popes engaged in untold brutalities to fulfill these objectives.

The Cathars, a peaceful and pious Christian sect who believed that humans are divine souls trapped in a material world created by an imperfect creator, were now marked by the Catholic hierarchy for annihilation. The crusade against them, a demonstration of Church ruthlessness and one of the most gruesome massacres in history started on July 22, 1209. What followed was horrific. The pogrom began in Béziers, in southern France. Some say that all the inhabitants were slaughtered in one week. Others put the number of dead at 40,000 men, women and children. During the first few days, 6,000 or 7,000 people were dragged to the Church of St. Mary Magdalene and executed.

Shamefully, condemnation of the Church's horrors against the Cathars, which lasted 45 years, has been subdued until recent times. Worse, there have been serious attempts to minimize the scope of this infamy and devalue the scale of the carnage to irrelevancy. Such efforts to suppress the truth seem to have bolstered the faith of those who wish to believe, against all reality, in the saintliness of the Church. The way mainstream Catholic writers now make light of this appalling event is unforgivable. The excuse that popes carried out these murders in the name of Christ is indefensible. If we accept the Church's explanation that crusaders were brave men who, imbued with deep religious sentiments, set out to punish people who veered away from conventional Christianity, then we are accepting an untruth. What is beyond doubt is that as soon as the Catholic armies were mobilized they became the most formidable killing machines Europe had ever known.

And that was just the beginning.

•

• •

From the earliest times, religion and politics become intimately intertwined. The cross-fertilization between statecraft and religious objectives leading to the manipulation of religious sensibilities for political purposes has a long and sordid history. Powerful individuals, most often high-ranking members of the clergy, ban essays, pamphlets and books viewed as anti-religious, particularly those that promote "secular humanism" (heresy), are deemed "seditious" (they utter inconvenient truths) or "obscene" (deeply offensive to feigned standards of decency). These multiple surges of inhibited thought combine to form a continuum of ignorance and irrationality that has a chilling effect on the dissemination of information and the exchange of rational ideas.

From *The Analects of Confucius* to *Harry Potter and the Sorcerer's Stone*, from Maimonides' *Guide to the Perplexed* to Thomas Paine's *The Age of Reason*, the *Popol Vuh* and the *Talmud*, *The Adventures of Huckleberry Finn* and *One Flew Over the Cuckoo's Nest*, from Voltaire's *Candide* to Huxley's *Brave New World*, thousands of books are banned, suppressed and censored on flimsy political, religious, sexual and social pretexts based on the tastes and beliefs of the dominant power structure of the moment. Ultimately, curtailment of free thought engulfs the mind in a sea of naïveté and absurdity that, abetted by the strident militancy of religion, persists to this day.

Medieval society struggles with arbitrary restrictions enforced by pressure groups not averse to subduing the timid, the unknowing and the pious with the blackjack tactics of intimidation, intellectual persecution, historical revisionism and the vilification of nonconformity. The expurgation of important ideas, compelling speculations and verifiable truths tacitly accepted by many, yet offensive to a vocal and influential minority, is widespread during the late Middle Ages. Censorship, propaganda, disinformation and the laundering of impressionable minds survive in various forms into modern times. If cogitation is intrinsic in man, so is, once his mind has been commandeered, his robotic rejection of concepts that elude him, defy his interpretation of reality, or undermine his social, political or religious stature.

Sometimes cloaked in symbolism, often flaunted with chilling realism, these lamentable human traits that the Church has so deftly manipulated would provide courageous artists, writers, philosophers and social activists endless grist for the anti-conformist mill. And, to the consternation of fantasy vendors, they would also delight in reminding the world that everything that is will cease to be.

AS DAWN ALIGHTS

DAWN ALIGHTS AND the pestilential haze of ignorance and stubborn attachment to absurd myths slowly begins to lift. A pale shaft of nascent self-awareness, a maturing consciousness of the natural world, spread little by little across Western Europe.

Gutenberg opens a print shop in Mainz. A goldsmith by trade, he is the first to use movable type printing and the originator of the mechanical printing press. His invention feeds the fledgling Renaissance and, as it greatly enhances scientific publishing, becomes a major catalyst for the ensuing scientific revolution. Troubled by the spread of knowledge (heresy) and always on the lookout for new sources of revenue, a papal court attempts to force printers to obtain a license. Inspired by this early form of extortion, the modern licensing system is far less interested in establishing norms of professional competency than in creating capital.

The first stock exchange begins trading in Antwerp.

Copernicus lays the foundations of astronomy and demonstrates the double movement of the planets -- rotation about their axes and revolution around the Sun. A century later, contradicting Biblical assertions (Psalms, Chronicles and Ecclesiastes) which insist that *"the world is firmly established, it cannot be moved,"* Galileo defends Copernicus' heliocentrism. Found "vehemently suspect of heresy" by the Roman Catholic Church, he is ordered imprisoned; the sentence is later commuted to house arrest.

Leonardo da Vinci, architect, painter, sculptor, writer, musician and engineer painstakingly develops the most accurate and comprehensive human anatomical chart. He visualizes the screw, the pulley, the articulated wing, the submarine, the helicopter and the armored assault vehicle long before practical uses are found for his ideas.

Concerned not with lofty ideals but with viable governance, the multi-talented Niccoló Machiavelli draws on his own experience and pens his famous satirical treatise on statecraft, *The Prince*. His reputation as a grey eminence or sinister political instigator is unfounded. "Machiavellism," the use of cunning and duplicity in politics, predates him. Man needs no instruction manual to sharpen his basest instincts.

Alart de Hameel, engraver and architect, supervises the erection of St. John's cathedral in 's-Hertogenbosch in the province of Brabant in the Low Countries. He completes the southern wing of the transept and begins work on the central nave. Lodges of operative masons flourish in the shadow of Europe's great castles and churches.

Erasmus, Dutch humanist, satirist and philosopher, examines the social and religious problems of his day with sobriety and logic. He criticizes popular Christian beliefs and infuriates Catholics and Protestants alike. He tries to establish a spiritual commonality on which

Catholics and Protestants can agree. His efforts earn him the ire of both camps.

Michelangelo, Rafael, Botticelli, Dürer create subtle and sophisticated visions that stir the imagination and awaken dormant or repressed emotions.

Bawdy, irreverent and politically incorrect, Cervantes and Rabelais turn fantasy, satire and the grotesque into an art form hitherto unequaled in literature.

Less than revered in his own lifetime, Shakespeare, by any other name, will be remembered as the greatest writer in the English language and the world's pre-eminent dramatist. Transparently anti-royalist and anti-clerical, his sometimes poignant, often scathing, always eloquent portraiture of kings, courtiers, nouveaux riches, simpletons and fools comes alive in his comedies and dramas.

Columbus stumbles upon a New World. His "discovery" forever alters the course of human events.

Antonie van Leeuwenhoek, the "father of micro-biology," invents the microscope. The breakthrough, and the findings it educes, will put an end to the belief of the time, that life is the result of God-mandated spontaneous generation. The microscope will later help dispel the notion that diseases are spawned in the "ether" -- the upper regions of Heaven -- are caused by *"mal aria"* (bad air) or are meted out by witches and evil spirits.

In that 100-year period that straddles the late Middle Ages and the early glows of the Renaissance is born, lives and dies an astute observer of human foibles and folly, an artist now recognized as the undisputed patriarch of Surrealism and, if the subtle and perplexing clues that season his eerie paintings are confirmed -- a member of an embryonic lodge of freethinkers, perhaps a forerunner of the Freemasons.

Is he the "notable artist" Jan van den Haag refers to in his letter? Neither Montvert nor Albeniz is ready to tally the allusions their Dutch correspondent offers without soliciting additional clues, however muted or guarded.

●

●　●

The Air France flight from Berlin eases on final approach to Charles de Gaulle Airport. Bone-tired and emotionally drained, Montvert thinks only of one thing: a well deserved, much needed weekend of rest.

He drives home, hidden reserves of energy guiding him mechanically on a course as familiar as it is tedious. Traffic is always heavy and slow. Spontaneous and inexplicable bottlenecks turn the A1 *autoroute* linking Roissy to Paris into a parking lot teeming with restless, horn-honking maniacs.

He reaches at last the *Périphérique*, the expressway that encircles Paris and provides principal points of entry into the once-walled City of Light. To his left, serene and timeless, the Sacré Coeur Basilica, its travertine stone domes and turrets glowing white, rises against a pale gray autumn sky.

Fed by memories of his youth, the spectacle never fails to evoke a cocktail of sensory responses.

Montmartre.

Frame by frame, he relives the moment. A cobbled

courtyard. Madame Muche, the concierge, ruddy-cheeked, feinting peevishness but susceptible to gallantry, sweeps the entranceway. A blue denim apron girds her opulent rotundity. A vague odor of fried onion wafts from her unshaven armpits.

"*Bonjour, Madame Muche.*"

"*Bonjour, jeune homme. Alors, l'école, ça va?*"

"*Tout va très bien, merci.* And how are things with you?"

"*Bof*, as you can see, a million chores, little time, only ten fingers." Josephine Muche props the broom handle against a broad, sallow cleavage and shows him the palms of her hands.

"Just look at them. Have you ever seen anything so pathetic?"

He mumbles words of commiseration and offers her some chocolate. *Suchard*. She blushes like a schoolgirl then scolds him softly.

"You shouldn't. I'm on a diet. My liver, you know." But she takes the offering and devours it all the same and the sugar triggers another burst of irascibility, this time aimed at her husband, Maurice, a burly, jovial Paris gendarme busy smoking a Gauloise.

"Some people have it easy," Josephine demurs, raising her eyebrows. "He's off today. You'd think he'd use his big muscles, the lunkhead, and help a little."

"Pay her no heed, *mon petit*," retorts Maurice, grinning. "It's pure theater. She should have been on stage, the woman. She's got enough talent for two, *n'est-ce-pas?*" Maurice spreads his arms, draws two semicircles in the air and cups his enormous hairy hands on the downward curve as if to enfold an imaginary pair of buttocks. Mortified, Madame Muche bites her lower lip, peers over her glasses and shakes an outraged finger at her husband. But outrage gives way to amusement and she surrenders a good-natured smile.

"*Ah, les hommes.* Men. They're all the same."

"Now, now, *mon amour.*" Maurice cowers with feigned terror. "Who loves his little Fifine? Her little Momo, *non?*" Madame Muche melts. They lay down their weapons and embrace. Monsieur Muche grabs Madame's generous posterior and declares with Gallic showmanship, "if that's not talent, I don't know what is...."

"Run for your life," exhorts Madame Muche. "This man is incorrigible. I'm liable to.... *Oh, la la!*"

Michel Montvert, then a star student at Paris's prestigious Ecole des Beaux Arts, remembers scaling four flights up a steep, creaking wooden stairway sagging from a century or more of clambering feet. Each narrow landing led to two small apartments with tiny rooms and eccentric plumbing. With each ascent, he embarked on a dizzying voyage up a spiral gullet resonating with discordant sounds and reeking with disparate exhalations, all vying for dominance. The fullness of their vitality haunts him still: He could smell Mademoiselle Vauclair's Friday fare -- cabbage soup, chicken gizzards and fried leeks. Madame Jabois' tremulous renditions of Mistinguett's classic, *Mon Homme*, (later reprised by Fanny Brice in *My Man),* echoed as she sloshed twice weekly in her Empire brass tub. Monsieur Vacheron's stentorian voice thundered like a summer storm as he barked at his eight-year-old daughter, Monique, over some petty infraction. Next door, Sylvie Lefèvre, homely and inhibited, stridently fended off her husband's accusations of infidelity with the butcher's errand-boy. Eugène Lefèvre knew his wife was incapable of disloyalty but morbid suspicion sharpened his libido and they eventually buried their sham conflict in furious and sonorous sex.

Mornings brought the redolence of croissants, evenings the aroma of freshly baked baguettes. Radios hummed in cacophonous unison, summarizing soccer scores, blasting the latest popular hits or reporting on the turmoil in Katanga (now Congo) or a smoldering conflict in some faraway place like Algeria and Indochina. He could hear the Golaud children repeating their verses in an exhausting drone as the garlic in Madame Morabito's *ailloli* and the commingling vapors of hearty wines and pungent beers wafted and settled in mid-air.

In this olfactory and sonic Babel also lived Wanda, her presence foretold by the heavy perfume she wore -- *Mitsouko by Guerlain* -- and the lugubrious wails she emitted at odd hours of the day and night, compliments of a mercifully discreet assortment of suitors. She had an unpronounceable Polish name so everyone called her "Mademoiselle Vanda" or "*l'anglaise*," even though she hailed from Steubenville, Ohio, via Tangiers and a dozen other Byronic locales, all weathered and abandoned in favor of Paris. Wanda was a tall, cadaverous middle-aged expatriate, the living caricature of castaways who squander their youth drifting from sleazy seaport to second-rate island resort in search of themselves.

Bedaubed with funereal make-up, she had an incurable American twang and a weakness for gin. Montvert had vainly tried to sharpen his English and often engaged her in conversation about Chicago and gangsters and cowboys and Indians and Hollywood and George Raft and James Cagney and New York's skyscrapers and Mark Twain's mighty Mississippi -- pretty much all he knew about America. But *"l'anglaise"* was either too drunk to contribute useful intelligence or she'd invariably insist on trading sex for the education Montvert longed for. He never took her up on it. A mixture of pity and revulsion made such commerce unlikely.

Only the Bredoux brothers -- Bernard and Bertrand -- veterans of *La Grande Guerre*, never married and subsisting on their pensions, lived in unsettling silence amid the dissonance and ubiquitous effluvia. They were kind-hearted souls with gentle smiles and simple truths, not given to idle chatter but always ready to comfort or encourage. He could see them now, their tall, lanky frames bent by age, a vague mustiness exuding from their taupe-colored cardigans, as they read the papers by the window. They had been generous with their baskets of green Normandy apples and steaming chestnuts. They had offered Montvert other gifts along the way: a small plaster bust of Hector Berlioz, a composer they described as "bombastic and annoying;" a tortoise shell cigarette case; a gold-nibbed fountain-pen; an illustrated first edition of Jules Verne's *Voyage to the Center of the Earth*.

Montvert had protested politely but they had insisted. "It'll be that much less to dust," they had quipped, winking at each other. "You're doing us a favor." It was a hint that held, in its subtlety, the promise of some impending finality the young art student did not have the maturity to decipher. He continued to do errands for them on rainy days or when the pain in their joints flared up. They never spoke about the Great War. He never asked. All wars, he surmised, possess a prosaic commonality, a tragic redundancy that make explication quite useless. It is the mark of great soldiers never to reminisce. Bernard and Bertrand committed suicide, Montvert later learned, when life, irrelevant and joyless, ceased to be worth living. They were found in bed, their medals and ribbons lying at the bottom of chamber pots in which they had dutifully, and with studied scorn for the military establishment, *La République* and posterity, taken their last crap. It was a scene straight out of Louis-Ferdinand Céline: blasphemy exalted by contempt.

Above the din and the intermingling scents, tucked away at the top of a narrow wooden corkscrew staircase, was home at last. It was in the nurturing silence of this sparsely furnished maid's quarters that he withdrew after school. Delivered from the world below, he'd hasten to the dormer, part the chintz curtains and gape at his city the way a boy covets a woman. Down below were the streets. He could read in their cadence like from an open diary and he reveled in the pantomimes they told. In the distance, Paris spread like a tapestry of gilded domes, verdant parks, esplanades, and ancient spires, and he'd marvel at the loveliness, the grace, long after twilight had draped the city in a star-studded mantle of lilac and periwinkle blue.

He'd then turn to his books. In their bosom, he explored the unrevealed nature of things, unearthing strange and wondrous emotions, toying with challenging abstractions. He wanted to conquer everything that is known and, if possible, to understand all that is unknowable. Such quest, he would discover, was as self-defeating as it was all-consuming. Alluring as they were, the voices behind the words (or was it the echo of his own ruminations?) invariably raised more questions than they answered. Curiosity is a long hallway filled with an infinite number of doors. Most never swing open, even at the loudest rap. He would conclude that to *seek* knowledge is the next best thing to *knowing*. In prospecting the unknown, he would also later concede, he was not as interested in acquiring new facts -- he was even less impressed with their utility or application -- as in how they played on his imagination, how they kindled heretofore unknown insights and sensations. Once digested, essential knowledge and fresh perspectives opened up a world of intimate feelings into which he withdrew the better to savor the transcendent realms they evoked. He was intent at all cost, and with each newly apprehended truth, to let his subconscious roam free. Knowledge was in vain unless it had the capacity to arouse an even greater thirst for what knowledge did *not* reveal. Art, to which he would devote his life, had no meaning unless it could beguile, stir, touch a chord, scandalize or stupefy. "Banality, however exquisitely rendered," he would say, "is the antithesis of art."

Surrealism, still in vogue in post-war Paris, played a pivotal role in this frenetic self-scrutiny. The eccentric cultural movement might have eluded him altogether had he not heard it stereotyped by opinionated know-it-alls as "intellectual snobbery" and "spiritual degeneracy," or dismissed as a *"hoax perpetrated by petty artists bent on scandalizing the purist mainstream."* Capricious condemnation of an idea, much more than praise, always aroused his curiosity. He often rallied around unpopular concepts or theories, not out of conviction, but contrariety.

Distracting society from its utilitarian yoke and reconciling irrationality with the rigors of conscious thought, a fundamental aim of Surrealism, found immediate favor with the wayward, nonconformist-in-training that Montvert was becoming. The works he read, the avant-garde paintings, sculptures and musical compositions he discovered along the way, produced an immediate and lasting joy, and he would eagerly surrender to their spell.

It was Baudelaire, his mother's favorite poet -- and one of France's most revered icons -- who introduced him to literary Surrealism. Aroused, he would acquire an enduring appreciation for the genre. The formidable bard lavished not only the perfect harmony of his verse on a young, hungry mind; his *Les Fleurs du Mal* also seemed to legitimize and vindicate Montvert's most visceral inclinations. Trusting neither man nor God, Baudelaire took refuge in primordial chaos, in the flesh, in orgiastic abandon. His verses crawl with monsters and freaks and pitiable *bas-monde* creatures all too reminiscent of ourselves. To set us at ease, to ensnare and disarm us perhaps, he stripped himself to the bone in a poignant display of self-deprecation. Like the haunting painting of Saint Sebastian by Rubens, Baudelaire flaunted the crimson gashes that scored his naked left breast to arouse not pity but indignation. He then agitated the demons, the ghouls that doze or stir within us, those we can never disavow. Shunned and lonely, the poet found redemption in the anonymity of crowds, among beggars, cripples, harlots, drunkards. In sad or worn faces, he discovered traces of fathomless drama, in ephemeral smiles a twinkling of hope deferred. His was the voice of all who love unrequitedly, suffer inconsolably, savor rare joys with touching intensity and endure the sorrows, the longings and broken dreams that clutter the deepest regions of our being. Unloved, perhaps unlovable, he drowned his wrath and his agony in alcohol and hashish, and he died at the age of 46, waiting for that which he knew would never come.

If Rimbaud and Poe, Baudelaire's contemporaries and partners-in-rhyme, gave madness a lyrical hue, it was Jean Cocteau, France's alchemical man, who urged Montvert up the winding stairway of Surrealism, who shepherded him across its portals, and eased him into its strange and wondrous inner sanctum. Cocteau's fairy tales, opium-induced phantasms and hallucinatory incantations imparted unique life to ambiguity, purpose to paradox.

"I am a lie doomed to always tell the truth."

Listening to Stravinsky's *Rite of Spring* and *The Firebird*, which he found exotic, erotic and delicious, Montvert gamboled and drowsed with Cocteau in fragrant fields of poppy only to awaken, sprinting in place in a relay race with himself. Forever seeking to jolt men out of their torpor as he himself prowled at the edges of delirium and paranoia, Cocteau's trails are strewn with scorn for the zealot, disdain for the hypocrite, contempt for the unimaginative, pity -- dark, raging, agonizing pity -- for those who feel, who ache, who weep as others pass them by unseeing, uncaring. Transfixed, Montvert often set sail on the wings of Cocteau's allegories, just to keep in shape. Every time he alit from these fantastic voyages he was reminded that rationality is no match for intuitiveness, that the imponderable can only be hinted at by appealing to the imagination, not common sense. No, Surrealists do not live in an ivory tower; it is their detractors who do, so Surrealists take careful aim instead and, with wit and irreverence, topple the flimsy edifice to the ground. With the dismal debris of their own intolerance now strewn at their feet, the victims of reality no longer recoil from it but acknowledge its ineffable absurdity. Once fathomed, Surrealism encourages its disciples to seek within themselves new dimensions, hidden planes of awareness. Surrealism is the vernacular of nonconformity. To some, it is the idiom of heresy.

Often, perhaps too often (some deemed such predisposition a solitary vice, like masturbation) Montvert turned to Franz Kafka, the supreme fabulist of modern man's cosmic predicament, for booster shots of melancholy and cynicism, the serums that deliver dreamers from groundless hope, idealists from pointless fancies. He meandered casually and without haste in

Joseph K's Escher-like labyrinths, ready to get lost, to become ensnared in the maddening plot, to merge into it. Kafka would bequeath a lifelong reflex and a healthy lack of forbearance for the meanness, the idiocy, the despotism of officialdom, the odious triviality of bureaucracy, the effrontery and intolerance of the ignorant, the shallow intellect and miserly pre-occupations of the petty bourgeois, the boorishness and vulgarity of the rabble, the sham majesty of upstarts.

Hardened by experience and an ebbing respect for authority, Montvert's expanding mixture of aversions would be reinforced by Nietzsche's warnings against mindless precepts and sordid rituals. What Montvert chose to distill from his florid orations is that helping dismember the tentacles of stupidity, dogma and prejudice [Maimonides called them "degenerate practices and senseless beliefs"] is a solemn obligation. Oh, how he struggled with Nietzsche. But he read on and reread *Thus Spake Zarathustra* and *The Anti-Christ* and *Twilight of the Gods*, and he dissected and agonized over every word, every twist of phrase, every last maze-like paragraph until Nietzsche's awesome genius erupted and lit up some heretofore dormant synapse inside his brain.

From Baruch Spinoza, his father's favorite philo-sopher (Henri Bergson came a close second) he learned to reject doctrines that don't make room for speculation or healthy skepticism; to view any truth that owes its existence solely to blind faith as a lie. Shackled to unbending creeds, afflicted with intellectual villainy and sloth, the contemporaries of Spinoza, a Dutch-born Marrano, shunned and rebuked him. The truth, Spinoza argued, can free humanity. He was referring to observable, verifiable and authenticated truth, not fabrications forced down people's throats.

"Immense pains have been taken to invest religion, whether true of false, with such pomp and ceremony, that it may rise superior to every shock and be always observed with studious reverence by the people."

Three hundred years later, Albert Einstein, when challenged to divulge his own religious convictions, sided with Spinoza, saying,

"I believe in Spinoza's God who reveals himself in the orderly harmony of what exists, not in a God who concerns himself with fates and actions of human beings."

Excommunicated by Jews, vilified by Christians, Spinoza was labeled a heretic and a rebel. His was an enviable malediction, Montvert mused, and he remembered vowing to emulate him in some way. It would take a more mature perusal of his work to recognize that he lacked both Spinoza's formidable intellect and his couth. He would have to settle for a Spinozan readiness to vex sacred cows, to invite hostility.

Voltaire, the freethinker whose moral code hinged on tolerance, generosity and a healthy dose of skepticism, was also required reading in school. Hostile to all metaphysics, Voltaire cautions with satirical ferocity against the perils of immoderation and groundless idealism. A believer in natural religion [based on reason and ordinary experience rather than the supernatural], he condemns the social effects of "revealed" doctrine, calling it "pernicious," and thus earning the everlasting antipathy of the Church.

"There can be no higher endorsement of one's real worth in a world of stunning hypocrisy," Montvert liked to say in his lectures, "than to invite such antagonism. It's infinitely more rewarding for an artist to be detested than ignored, to die at the hands of his enemies than to bask in the cold light of public acclaim."

Orwell's view of freedom -- "the right to tell people what they *don't* want to know" appealed to him intuitively. But it was the stirring humanism of Victor Hugo and Emile Zola, their preoccupation with the unlearned lessons of history that strengthened Montvert's decision to startle the smug and the compliant, to challenge the established order, to prophesy chaos and decay as a hedge against their inevitability. Hugo and Zola celebrated the enormous power of passionate, hard-hitting truth-telling. Their prose was poetry. Their polemics were honed to sing and sting and move men to great deeds, and occasionally drive them to infamy, shame and remorse. Montvert, who can sniff traces of insincerity and connivance in the words of politicians and popes alike, would quickly learn that the "truth" is nothing more than the most persuasive of two or more conflicting doctrines, and that the urge by some to exhume it is habitually frustrated by the reflex of others to keep it entombed.

●

● ●

All his mentors were there at his beck and call, lovingly shelved in alphabetical order, ready to impart fresh insights, to titillate, amuse and exhort, astound and stir at every turn of the page. They kept him company when homework was done or postponed as he waited for the girls to climb to his old drafty garret. It was in the sagacity of books, in their wit and nonconformity that he trusted most. And it was in their company that he withdrew long after the girls had left and lust, now assuaged, yielded to more cerebral cravings and to the greater dividends of sleep, alone at last, in his very narrow bed.

●

● ●

He had rearranged the room, pushing the bed against the sloping skylight so he could gaze at his beautiful Paris, like from an aerie, as he made love to nubile maidens with violet-scented lips, sprigs of *muguet*, lily of the valley, adorning their tangled tresses, and as antimony clouds sailed across lavender skies.

Freckle-faced and deliciously depraved, sixteen-year-old Ginette, the concierge's daughter, had taught him things only a freshly deflowered nymphet will dare. Free of shame or pretense, spurred by precocious sensuality, she had granted him every whim, indulged every caprice. They had performed elaborate acrobatics to the accompaniment of Ravel's *Daphnis and Chloe*, contriving to climax simultaneously as the Bacchanale's joyous finale rose to a rapturous crescendo. Blissfully exhausted, they would then settle back against a large down pillow and read from Guillaume Apollinaire's erotic novellas, *The Adventures of a Young Rakehell* and *The Debauched Hospodar*, parodies of the sizzling French novels circulated in secret in Victorian England. Ginette was especially fond of the well-endowed Romanian nobleman, Prince Mony Bibescu, whose insatiable urges had taken him from the Paris bordellos to the bath-houses of the Orient in a never-ending quest for the ultimate orgasm. Aroused by the prince's improbable exploits, they would start all over again.

Once a month or so, with Ginette gone for weekend visits to her *mémée* in Auvergne, it was a fellow student, Isabelle -- "la belle" -- blue-blooded and demure, the niece of a high-ranking member of the French Senate, who looked in on Montvert. Refined, exuding a breeding found only in old money tirelessly replenished, Isabelle had deemed Ravel's ballet too long. So they had settled for Debussy's ten-minute transcendental *Prélude à l'Après-Midi d'un Faune*. Ten minutes was all Isabelle could grant him anyway. His recitations of the most grotesque passages of De Sade's *Justine* and *Juliette*, some redolent of sodomy and scatology, followed by the gyrations and undulations he exacted as she rode astride him at the edge of the bed, often made her nauseous. She once vomited all over him. He never quite felt the same about Isabelle's patrician little *derrière* after that. He continued to see her now and then because she *shlepped* all the way from courtly Le Vésinet to the plebeian escarpments of Montmartre just to get laid. Such servility in a highborn, Montvert felt, could only be rewarded with basic, crude fornication.

He eventually lost both Ginette and Isabelle, the result of an indiscretion with a third *p'tite amie*, Elyse, whom he had picked up at a magazine kiosk on Place Blanche as he rummaged for his favorite old comics. Elyse liked the accordion. He did too, but over fish and chips and cold fermented cider in a cozy bistro at dusk on the banks of the Marne River, not as an attendant to fucking. So they had each other in silence, lulled by gentle rains or cooing doves perched atop the gargoyles. Of humble birth and uninhibited, like Ginette, Elyse gave her all, anytime, anywhere without the slightest affectation. She giggled a lot. He'd read Rimbaud and Verlaine, and she'd nestle her head in the crook of his shoulder like a kitten and she'd stray, her eyes fixed upon his moving lips, a moistened finger buried between her thighs, her thoughts drifting on the wings of the poets' magic incantations.

There had been others. Nothing was left of them now but the dim memory of an ephemeral romance.

And then, one day, as he perused an encyclopedia of medieval art, Montvert stumbled on -- no, rediscovered -- a Flemish painter, the same polemicist that had enthralled him as a boy. The experience was to have a profound effect on his artistic proclivities, on his career and on a sequence of events in which he would play a prominent role.

•

• •

Back in his apartment on Rue la Boêtie, in the fashionable 8th Arrondissement, Montvert lets out a deep sigh of relief. He drops his attaché case on the vestibule floor, next to the Ming planter that now doubles as an umbrella stand, and hangs his raincoat on the cherry-wood portemanteau. He unloosens his tie, crosses a spacious living room festooned with treasures: Chagall, Miró, Magritte, Perahim, Max Ernst, Zadkine and a signed replica of Brancusi's exquisite *Bird in Flight*. In the bedroom, he kicks his shoes off, tosses his jacket on the divan and places his watch on the dainty Louis XV gilt-edged cherry wood chest of drawers. He peers for a moment at his beloved Ucello, bought at an auction in Milan. Ucello was a 15th century painter who skillfully tricked the senses, compelling the viewer to mistake illusion for reality. His battle scenes are wholly improbable tangles of horses, riders, lancers, pennants, helmets, and scraps of landscape, with each element fitting elegantly in a perfect abstract geometry. For Montvert, who is fond of metaphor and abhors literalism, abstraction, innuendo and geometry flouted are the essence of artistic activism.

•

• •

Montvert showers, changes into casual wear, goes down to his corner bistro and orders a double espresso and a croissant. In the paper he reads that a Bush administration memorandum had once asserted that federal funds can subsidize groups that discriminate based on religion and hire only people of a certain faith. He briefly congratulates himself for living in France and proceeds to call Albeniz on his cell phone.

"Manuel?"

"*Si.*"

"It's me, Michel. I'm back. I read the letter."

"Good. What do you think?"

"You were right. It is *intriguing*. But van den Haag's clues about the alleged author of the document, while tantalizing, are vague. I've come up with several potential candidates, none I'd stake my reputation on -- and that's assuming van den Haag is telling the truth."

"I've indulged in conjecture too," Albeniz says, "and I think I know who van den Haag is alluding to. Who do you have in mind?"

"Well, Hans Memling and Gerard David, to start. But Memling was German and David, although an early Flemish painter, was heavily influenced by Memling. He was a disciple, not a forerunner. His themes hardly fit the stylistic radicalism van den Haag describes."

"I agree. Who else?"

"The great Cranach the Elder, but he too was German and the time frame doesn't match. Hans Baldung Grün came to mind. His lascivious *"Witch and Dragon,"* which combines lechery and the grotesque, foreshadows a break with religious themes but, again, he was from Swabia and he resided and worked in Strasbourg. Van Eyck was a Dutchman, but he lived much earlier than our mystery challenger. The incomparable Dürer, yet another German, lived later. Giovanni Bellini comes close, but he was Italian and his paintings were influenced by the Venetian School. De' Barbari's striking portrait of Fra Luca Pacioli, in which he demonstrates a theorem by Euclid, is filled with what appears to be Masonic symbolism but his method and style, not to mention his nationality, disqualify him as well."

"Anyone else, Michel?"

"Yes. There's one last pretender, a remarkable trendsetter I have always admired. It's a long shot but everything in van den Haag's cryptic missive seems to point to him. I'm almost certain it's...."

"Don't say it," Albeniz interjects." Let's savor what must remain a tempting inference until van den Haag lets the cat out of the bag. Write him and tell him we're interested. I've checked his Masonic affiliations. He's on the level. I don't know what this will lead to. But if the author of the document turns out to be who we think he is, if the contents of that document contradict what four hundred years of sheer speculations claim to reveal about the man -- and if we expose what could have been a myth, if not a hoax -- we'll raise a *"santa batahola,"* how do you say in French, a *"chambard,"* a big stink...."

Montvert smiles broadly. He's never shied away from controversy. The prospect of raising a big stink in the interest of truth, the integrity of artistic expression and the satisfaction of his own impish iconoclasm fills him with delight.

"De acuerdo, Manuel. I'll tell van den Haag we've agreed to help and ask him to tell us more. I'll be in touch

as soon as I hear from him. *Hasta luego, querido hermano."*
   "Igualmente."

●

● ●

Michel Montvert, *né* Greenberg, the grandson of
Romanian Jewish émigrés, is beaming. He's done the
math. If the contentious document was embargoed until
five hundred years after the artist's death -- that is in 2016
-- then the artist must have died in 1516. Both Bellini and
De' Barberi were tempting choices: they died that year.
But they were Italian, not Flemish. Only one "notable"
painter matches van den Haag's sketchy intimations, a
Master hailed as an "inventor" by his contemporaries
and recognized as having had an indelible influence on
parody and on modern art, notably Surrealism. And
Montvert, an acclaimed expert on the genre, is certain he
knows who that *inventor* is.

ECCE HOMO?

THE INVENTOR LEAVES behind a mesmerizing collection of masterpieces. Yet little is known of him. The most inscrutable painter of the 15th century, his bizarre, disquieting renditions elicit volumes of psycho-babble. His legendary creations fascinate, startle, shock and often horrify. Art historians admit they know close to nothing about the man himself. Only dogged efforts to solve the mystery that surrounds him and gritty detective work allow, with wide gaps and missing links along the way, to reconstitute a few key dates and salient details, all of which must be read and plumbed against the religious, social, political and philosophical backdrop that was the artist's world.

Born with another surname than that by which he is more widely known, he comes into the world in October 1453. He changes his name, adopting the last syllable of his hometown, 's-Hertogenbosch. His death in 1516 is recorded in the register of the Brotherhood of Notre Dame, in which he is inducted in 1486. A funeral mass in his memory is held in the famed St. John Cathedral where a menagerie of grotesque ornaments adorns the exterior façade and the choir.

In 1488, also according to the archives of the Brotherhood, he presides over the "Swan's Banquet," a ritual said to have inspired his baffling painting, *Marriage at Cana*, source of much debate about his Masonic identity. That same year he is raised a Master. Scant other facts survive. He marries a "woman of landed gentry," completes a matrix for stained glass windows in the Brotherhood's lodge at St. John Cathedral, and dies. His funeral is recorded with laconic detachment. He leaves behind no letters or diaries. Nothing is known about his personality, his thoughts on the meaning of life, his raison d'être as an artist and social satirist. Whatever might have existed is presumed lost or, more characteristically, deliberately destroyed by the artist to ensure privacy or deter the uninitiated from decoding the mysterious clues his life and work could have left behind. Another theory explored by Montvert in a monograph published in the Annals of the Museo del Prado in Madrid suggests that the painter's most disturbing works were purchased en masse after his death, less out of reverence for his genius than out of fear that they present graphic and damaging allusions about a bloated aristocracy and a corrupt clergy, two self-anointed elites who have made it a career of oppressing and exploiting the masses.

Montvert's assumptions are greeted with cautious interest by the Spanish art world. Miffed, the Archdiocese of Madrid issues a frosty statement accusing Montvert of engaging in wild conjectures that are unsupported by history.

"Whose 'history'," Montvert asks. His question is ignored.

•

• •

Around 1475, at a time when the artist's career begins to blossom, painters of the day conform to immutable principles laid out long before them. Their pictures are infused with the solemnity and stiffness of divine service. They retrace Biblical events and are contrived to invite the faithful to humble devotion and mystic exaltation of the soul. The flock is beckoned to higher spirituality but the language, which the flock must grasp without ambiguity, is banal, prosaic. It commands blind obedience to God; it discourages self-scrutiny and condemns profane knowledge. Submit. Kneel. Bow your head. Pray. Believe. Believe or else.

The painter Montvert and Albeniz suspect van den Haag is referring to in his letter is the first to break away from this tradition. With him, art begins to shake off the rigid tutelage of the Church. Outwardly pious, his paintings also point fingers at the clergy's debauchery and inventive cruelty. Man is no longer God's finest enterprise but a weak, flawed creature given to extremes of naïveté and ferocity, charity and malice, creativity and nihilism.

Revered or reviled, the "inventor's" paintings are hard to describe, except for the obvious which, more often than not, conveys obscure or allegorical concepts. Underplayed but ubiquitous, alchemy, magic, the Kabbalah, Scripture, augury and folk humor unite to create strange, sometimes frightening, always other-worldly scenes of trancelike boredom or hysteria. Set against deceptively tranquil backdrops, his triptychs and wood panels erupt in paroxysms of perversion and lunacy. Miscegenated creatures excrete gold, fly in satanic formations to monstrous Sabbaths where they devour unspeakable fare. They retch, pray with trancelike fervor, lust after sexless hybrids, assault and kill and in turn die a thousands deaths skewered by the very wind instruments on which they play their lugubrious tunes. Everywhere, someone inflicts or surrenders to untold abominations with a detachment akin to apathy while fantastic beings, part-animal, part-ghoul, tear at their flesh or render them mad. Somewhere, lost or bewildered, they reach out, clutching at something, sometimes at themselves, as if to shake off some invisible yet intolerable yoke. And they never let go.

The Master's brush conveys stupefaction, bestiality, innocence and crushing ennui. Through his tormented gaze are reflected all the expressions that betray the madcap ambivalence of the human spirit. Sensuality and eroticism, sometimes veiled, often explicit, saturate his images but there is no passion in the coveting, no humanity in the piety, no fervor in the carnality. Depraved as they seem, his characters inspire pity, not horror. Pervasive, often gratuitous, scenes of widespread violence are offset by the lifeless gaze of both tormentor, who shows no fury and victim, who appears to feel no pain. Their ordeal, gruesome as it is, never seems to convey an explicit level of intolerability. All are dazed, stunned. When one suffers, the great painter tells us as we gape at the numb or snarling expressions of his subjects, it's just a question of degree. Pain travels but it never goes away.

•

• •

A late October downpour drenches Paris. The rain turns to swirling tendrils of vapor that rise skyward as soon it reaches the ground. The City of Light, resplendent under azure skies, acquires the kind of glossy murkiness that gives films noir their tantalizing and ill-omened ambiance. The weather lends an eerie backdrop to the movie Montvert is watching on TV, the dark, caustic *Le Silence de la Mer*. Based on an anti-German novel secretly published in occupied France, the brooding, sparsely dialogued psychodrama evokes long forgotten childhood memories. He had seen it once before, when he was ten or so, with his parents in a theater in Marseille. And, some of the scenes, he remembers, had stirred recollections of yet earlier events that had marked him forever.

Strewn on the settee is an assortment of letters and packages received in the morning mail. Montvert absent-mindedly sifts through his correspondence. He recognizes a distinctive handwriting and unseals an envelope.

Dear Brother Montvert,

I received your kind letter this morning. Heartened by your encouraging tenor and the interest you share with Dr. Albeniz in this matter, I hasten to reply.

First, to allay some of your misgivings, let me reassure you that my ancestor's posthumous commentaries are models of clarity. He doesn't mince words. His feelings and convictions are bluntly articulated. From them can be distilled the crucial premises upon which his works are based: Sin and folly are the universal legacy of mankind; hell-fire through intolerance, greed and war its common destiny. This deeply gloomy perspective, however emblematically conveyed, must not be confused with mysticism, which he rejected, or fire-and-brimstone religiosity, which he abhorred. Contrary to the grandiloquent assertions of scholars who, for lack of evidence or imagination, see him as a docile agent of Christian doctrine, nothing in this astonishingly candid tract (or in his paintings, for that matter) betrays even a shred of personal spiritual conviction. His insights into the human soul are hard-nosed and grounded in experience and observation. As you will note when you peruse the document, his language -- like much of his art -- is laced with irony, anticlerical verve, and spiked with acerbic satire against the Church. He denounces the corruption and hypocrisy of the clergy, the repressive power of the papacy. Craving for truth, longing to expose it, he joins his contemporaries in protest against the abuses, against simony, against bribery, against the commerce of indulgences, against the scorching venality of God's emissaries.

The most provocative aspect of my forebear's

work, once initial consternation or shock subsides, lay in the symbolism, at times subdued, often manifest, that suggests he was a member of a sect of free-thinkers, most probably -- as you put forward in your essay published in the Travaux du Grand Orient of France -- a precursor of our Fraternal Order. His elegantly penned testament puts an end to the speculation. He confirms his association with organizations that, while only vaguely reminiscent in structure and scope of modern Freemasonry, led a double life and whose covert objective was to challenge the repressive influence of religion on scholarship and personal freedoms.

Last, yes, I am the final descendant of Jeroen Van Aken, better known as Hieronymus Bosch.

Copies of his manuscript are being sent to you and Dr. Albeniz by air courier. Please let me hear from you after you've had a chance to peruse and digest this astonishing opus. I thank you in advance for consenting to help shed *Further Light* on the man and his edifying pronouncements.

Looking forward to laboring with you and Brother Albeniz in the very near future, I remain, for Reason,

Fraternally yours,

Jan H. van den Haag, 32°.

MYTHBUSTERS

FELIX QUI POTUIT *Rerum Cognoscere Causas.* Happy is he who penetrates the secret nature of things.

I, Jeroen van Aken, also known as Hieronymus Bosch, painter by trade, hereby affirm on my honor, that the account that follows is factual and that the views it expresses are mine, offered therein unhindered by outside influence or coercion, and penned in the twilight days of my life to remove any doubt that might arise after my death as to my convictions, penchants and the meaning and aim of my humble harvest.

I am indebted to heredity, most especially to my grandfather Jan and my father Anthonius for what my peers generously regard as a skill. It is to the human condition, filled with naïve aspirations and irresistible cravings, hopeless dreams and inevitable nightmares, poetry and vulgarity, gallantry and cowardice, innocence and wickedness, compassion and evil, and to the ravages of time that I owe my inspiration. The Reformation, counter-Reformation and the Inquisition have perforce also educed heretofore pent-up emotional responses against the rigid credos and strict religious doctrines used to manipulate the mind and ensnare the soul.

Naturally inclined to favor men in the pursuit of carnal pleasure, I married a fine woman whose character and reputation ensured mine against unwelcome scrutiny and spiteful tongues. She gave me a son and a daughter who, brimming with filial love, showed, like their mother, neither a passion for art, an appetite for independent reasoning or a lust for knowledge. Time will swallow them in its dark abyss but perhaps one of their descendants will awaken, blessed with curiosity and imagination, and dedicated to the dissemination of truth.

Although temperamentally reclusive, it is my sensuality and partialities that have caused me to seek the company of men and to join the Brotherhood of Notre Dame. It is there that I met open-minded fellows who, like me, found in it a forum in which the rational exploration of unorthodox concepts could openly take place without arousing the suspicion of our spiritual overseers and subjecting us to their murderous wrath. Some of my companions, given to uninhibited erotic pursuits, formed a secret guild, instituting our own rituals, emblems and modes of recognition. We called ourselves Adamites in mock commemoration of man's "original" innocence and to recreate what must surely have been a time of orgiastic abandon in heaven and on earth.

One of my triptychs memorializes this shame-free epoch. The bawdy scene in the center panel does not censure -- as many believe -- unrestrained sensual pleasure. On the contrary, it extols earthly delights that are publicly denounced by keepers of morality who luxuriate in them when no one looks. The left panel satirizes the glorified image people have of a fictitious Paradise. The right one parodies the earthly Hell the Church does not want us to envisage: a present-day underworld in which hedonism and cruelty and the hypocrisy of conformist orthodoxy rule.

To posterity, which is given to wild inferences when it is not seeking to discredit or pay gratuitous homage, let it be known that I have chosen not to sign several of my paintings. Some were executed under my guidance or completed by worthy apprentices. Others, I felt, implicit in their eccentricity and plainspoken scorn for the usurpers of minds and souls, threatened to expose me as an apostate, a conniver or an agent of Satan.

Being a confirmed atheist, I hold that individuals should never accept concepts proposed as truth without recourse to proof and sound reasoning. I strive to erect my convictions on the basis of fact, common sense and observation. I reject the intellectually castrating custom of relying on "conventional wisdom," popular culture, legend and reflex rituals imposed by the ruling classes to dogmatize society and keep the rabble quiet. I believe that given known facts, cogent inference and logic, there is no evidence to support the existence of supernatural phenomena. I further hold as evil the force-feeding of deviant and absurd beliefs upon the ignorant and simple-minded.

Advocates of inflexible dogma are especially skillful at blurring the truth or shielding against the glare of irrefutable fact. The greater their zeal in defending their causes, or silencing their rivals, the more tempting it becomes for them to assert that erudition, intellectualism, the pursuit of Light and iconoclasm are sinister cabals designed to spread impious or discomfiting ideas. Their mendacity and evil schemes must be exposed.

We all defy mortality according to our nature. Some spend their lives indulging in mindless diversions. Consumed with arrogance, using force of arms, wielding the mighty Cross, others bully people into submission. Others yet, labor to make a statement, to leave a permanent record of their brief existence. I paint. My work is my proclamation.

It is my last wish and command that future generations, should time and wisdom fail to cure the folly of blind faith and degenerate customs, be reminded of the horrors I have witnessed and, in time, be delivered from the scourge of fixed and aberrant ideas.

In the accompanying appendices I attempt to shed light on the attitudes and moral dilemmas that inspired works I credit as my own. In them, I also endeavor to convey my personal conviction that any truth that owes its existence, not to rational examination or logical deduction, but to blind faith is a wretched lie. Force me to believe and you feed my incredulity.

Executed this 7 February 1516.
Hieronymus Bosch, painter.

•

•   •

Vitam Impendere Vero. To consecrate life to the truth.
"Are you a Mason?"
"My Brothers recognize me as such."
"What does Freemasonry strive for?"
"Enlightenment and the betterment of man."
"Where do you labor?"
"In a lodge called the Middle Chamber."
"Are you a Master?"
"The acacia is known to me."
"What did you learn?"
"I was first taught to know myself. I was then led to the study of arts and sciences valuable to society, useful to my evolution as a man and indispensable to my development as a Freemason."
"What moral lessons did you draw from this knowledge?"
"I understood that learning is vital to man, that it plants in us the seed of all virtues, that it unites us and that it reveals in each of us his rights and obligations."
"What allegorical significance does the degree of Master Mason impart?"
"It recreates the intolerance against knowledge and it epitomizes the everlasting struggle waged by Truth against ignorance, fanaticism and superstition."
"For what purpose was the grade of Master created?"

"To fight bigotry, the enemy of knowledge and enlightenment, and to exalt the Truth."

"Does this struggle entail risks and perils?"

"Yes, because the dissemination of Truth has political consequences."

What do you mean?"

"The Truth is a source of anxiety that inevitably threatens certain centers of worldly power."

"How old are you?"

"Seven and more."

"What does this allude to?"

"Seven and more is an indeterminate number that symbolizes wisdom and the Master Mason's level of maturity. It also reminds us that the more we learn, the more we realize how very little we know."

"Thank you, my Brother. The Lodge will now recess and reconvene to hear and deliberate the presentation Brother Montvert has kindly consented to prepare for this meeting."

The Brothers rise to their feet, gather around the altar and, in due form, exclaim, "Houzzai, Houzzai, Houzzai. Liberté, Egalité, Fraternité."

•

•   •

On November 2 -- All Saints Day -- flanked by Manuel Albeniz who flies in from Madrid, Michel Montvert a 32nd degree Master Mason, addresses a specially convened meeting of the Charles Darwin Lodge, an affiliate of the Grand Orient of France in Paris.

"Venerable Master, distinguished officers, my fellow Masons: Through an extraordinary confluence of events, my esteemed Brother and colleague, Dr. Manuel Albeniz and I recently came into possession of an astonishing document that we have since expertly and categorically authenticated. Made available by a Brother in Holland who has requested anonymity, and reaching across the centuries, the document is penned and signed by a celebrated artist whose paintings continue to intrigue, startle and inspire. More astounding yet, our Dutch correspondent claims to be the last descendant of that inimitable painter. After diligent research, we have concluded that there is no reason to doubt his sincerity. The painter I refer to is called El Bosco in Spain, Jerôme Bosch in France and is otherwise universally known as Hieronymus Bosch.

"I have before me a facsimile of the original document and I shall proceed to read from the extraordinary and illuminating preamble. An appendix in which the author discusses the underlying principles and rationale for nine of his most recognizable paintings is far too long to examine at this time. A copy will be available online and in our library."

Standing west of the altar, on which rests a book of blank pages, emblematic of the faith -- or lack of faith -- of the assembled Brothers, Montvert, in a cadenced and steady voice, reads from the extraordinary document. His audience is mesmerized.

•

• •

"In conclusion, my Brothers, Hieronymus Bosch continues to defy the copious speculations of art critics and psychologists. Like us, he remains true to his central mission: the denunciation of censorship, thought control, whether political or religious, and other encroachments on personal freedoms that prevent people from accessing information, sharing controversial ideas and articulating opinions deemed to be discomfiting or even hostile to an almighty and ruthless oligarchy.

"Contrary to the faulty deductions or deliberate deceptions foisted on the public by various scholars, Bosch does not reaffirm his Christian orthodoxy. His work, now we know, is an incisive social commentary, more precisely an indictment against the ignominy of forced ideas and the absurdity of irrational beliefs that Descartes would expand upon less than one hundred years later in his famous *Discours*. The subdued melancholy of Bosch's words suggests his work is also an ode to the beauty and wretchedness of human existence. He also reminds us that those who would manage our lives, religious and secular, will not hesitate to falsify the truth, concoct lies and suppress criticism to protect their own interests or the alleged well being of those they pretend to govern. As history confirms, we can no longer assume that the monitoring of eccentric ideas and the application of retaliatory gag rules, always harsh and despotic, are to be found solely in the Dark Ages or in some Orwellian realm, or that they emanate from the deepest recesses of some imaginary clandestine government-within-a-government. Targets of both Nazi and "communist" persecution, committed to defending our secular ideals, which include absolute separation of Church and State, we Freemasons know that intolerance is rife even in self-described democratic states where it often assumes a pernicious character, that it is spawned and fed by ideological bullies, deranged zealots, political shock troops, churches, school boards, partisan community newspapers, libraries and fascist groups that attack with malicious sanctimony any concept that eludes them or that threatens their *modus vivendi*."

●

● ●

A carefully edited copy of Montvert's remarks and the entire text of Bosch's foreword are published in the prestigious *Travaux* of the Grand Orient de France and reprinted in the proceedings of constituent lodges around the world. A transcript, as are major Grand Orient communications destined for public consumption, is forwarded to the influential left-of-center daily, *Le Monde*, and, out of courtesy, to the darling of the French right, *Le Figaro*. The editor of *Le Monde*, a member of another Grand Orient lodge, tactfully runs the piece on Page Seven. The headline is restrained but telling:

De l'au-delà, un célèbre peintre Flamand
met en garde contre les abus de l'Eglise
(From the hereafter, a famed Flemish artist
warns against the abuses of the Church)

Le Figaro, whose motto is, "*Without the right to criticize there can be no true praise,"* refuses to publish the article.

A few days later, under a banner headline screaming **IGNOBLE!**, *Le Calvaire,* (The Calvary) the conservative French Catholic weekly magazine, issues a riposte that targets secularism, Freemasonry and *"some of our brethren of the Mosaic Faith,"* accusing them *of "giddily conspiring to falsify history, vilify the Church, undermine Christianity and demoralize the flock."*

Montvert and Albeniz are over the moon. Their jubilation is short-lived. They realize, as Albeniz had predicted, that they have opened a can of worms -- raised "a big stink" that will prove difficult to ventilate.

The Vatican, characteristically reticent, withholds comment but is not inactive. Pope Benedict summons his top lieutenants in the Curia and the Congregation for the Doctrine of the Faith. One of them recommends that the Holy See issue an encyclical *"that unambiguously telegraphs our views on the matter."* The pontiff rejects the idea.

"We cannot appear to be reacting from a position of weakness. We must communicate our displeasure with utmost poise and decorum. This is still a local issue." The pope shakes his head with impatience. "Ah, the French.... Let's first work through the Paris archdiocese. Perhaps Trente-Trois and his boys can defuse the situation."

•

• •

At the behest of André Trente-Trois, Archbishop of Paris, Bishop Jean-Marie Touvier, his special envoy, calls Montvert and requests an urgent and secret summit. He asks that the tête-à-tête be held in the sacristy of the Saint-Etienne-du-Mont Church. Montvert, who has a wicked sense of humor, wisely refrains from suggesting Saint Sulpice Church, made famous by The Da Vinci Code. Instead, he proposes that they meet at Copernicus Lodge, temporarily "dark," or inactive, as it undergoes renovation. Reluctantly, Bishop Touvier agrees.

The meeting is hastily convened and held on the evening of November 5th. Facing Bishop Touvier are Pierre Mandel, Master of Copernicus Lodge, Michel Montvert, Manuel Albeniz and Jacques Lelouch, Grand Master of the Grand Orient of France. The editor of *Le Monde*, claiming a prior engagement, declines the invitation.

●

● ●

"Gentlemen," Bishop Touvier begins with all the aplomb his high office confers, "the Holy Father is saddened and troubled. The article in *Le Monde* has upset a number of high-ranking prelates in France and in Rome who have called for a strong and unambiguous response. The pope has asked for calm and patience but he is adamant. The Grand Orient of France must apologize. Freemasons have no business harassing us. You must also persuade *Le Monde* to issue a retraction. The article has all the makings of a very tall tale, a thrilling one at that, but a tall tale nonetheless that is apt to confuse, unnerve and dishearten many Catholics, and...."

"With all due respect, your Excellency, let me be clear," Montvert cuts in. "One, we can present you with irrefutable evidence of the authenticity of the document reproduced in *Les Travaux* and later reprinted in *Le Monde*. Two, the Grand Orient of France is under no obligation to apologize to an institution that has maligned Freemasonry through the ages, repeatedly attempted to destroy it and continues to excoriate it both in official papal pronouncements and homilies in churches around the world. Three, the business of Freemasonry is to ferret out the truth and to circulate it. Four, we have no influence on what a newspaper may or may not publish, nor would we exert it if we did. Freedom of expression is a prized entitlement in this country. The very fact that *Le Figaro* declined to run the story offers ample proof of media independence.... Last, *Le Monde* readers, all left-of-center, are not likely to be confused, unnerved or disheartened by a tract that echoes their innermost convictions. Nor should what will surely be the brief resurrection of a largely unknown painter cause devout Catholics to defect."

"We don't fear defections," Bishop Touvier exclaims. "We fear the destabilizing effect of confusion on the soul."

"Confusion," Albeniz interjects. "What confusion? Sixty-six percent of the French are nominally Catholics, but they're more French than Catholic. Their piety is largely ceremonial, perfunctory, sustained by habit and reflex, not unshakable conviction. Growing discontent

with the meddlesome influence of the Church of France
-- the 'Vatican's *eldest daughter*' -- on secular education,
and its persistent efforts to influence politics continue to
bolster French support for the absolute and categorical
separation of Church and State our nation enjoys. Most
Frenchmen have never heard of Hieronymus Bosch.
Those who may be vaguely familiar with his name aren't
about to loose sleep over his art or its hypothetical
influence on society, past or present."

"Maybe," Touvier protests, "but this latest bombshell
suggests that the world of art, represented by Monsieur
Montvert and you, Dr. Albeniz, and abetted by the
Grand Orient of France, are keen on disrupting this
blissful lack of interest and, in so doing, on kindling
renewed antipathy toward the Church."

"That's nonsense and you know it," Montvert snaps
back. "The world of art is focused on art, not on faith,
even if faith sometimes inspires art. Religious art is *art*;
worldly art is *art*. Some is great, some is not. Much of it is
quite forgettable. But what artists say in their work,
allegorically or literally, is their business. Who but the
Church or some despotic government would dare
impugn their freedom of conscience or prevent them
from exercising it as they see fit? No one has ever
ridiculed Michelangelo's sublime Pieta, Murillo's
enchanting Annunciation or Grünewald's heart-
wrenching Crucifixion. All who love art stand in awe of
these geniuses, of their power to delight, inspire or
agitate. But when Bosch or El Greco or Dali or Picasso or
Klimt or Munch explore the genre and offer an eccentric
or deconstructionist perspective of the same subjects, the

Church cries foul. Only traditionalist art is decent, it insists, only God-inspired compositions have the power to stir the soul. Modernism is crude, degenerate, unintelligible. It lacks the poignancy of sacred works.... If the Church had focused on its own spirituality instead of hijacking the masses and reducing them to paralytic stupor, it might have avoided the kind of hostility centuries of dogmatism and intolerance have wrought."

"As for Freemasonry, and more specifically the Grand Orient of France," Grand Master Lelouch hastens to add, "we're not interested in restraining religious freedom. You should know that by now. Your office has spent years scrutinizing Freemasonry. So have your predecessors. All you've managed to do, without having ever stepped inside a lodge, is to regurgitate hackneyed falsehoods -- that our rituals are a distortion of the Christian sacrament and that, irreligious libertines that we are, we promote social anarchy. Freemasons come in all shapes and sizes and colors and ethnicities and religious convictions. Some are deeply spiritual. Others openly profess their agnosticism or atheism. We embrace them all. What we strive for is intellectual maturity and flexibility, enlightenment, a passion for knowledge and a scrupulous respect for truth, social equality and justice."

"No." Touvier objects, raising an admonitory finger. "Only by surrendering to God can man secure these blessings. Instead, the subversive forces of secularism, backed by Marxists and Freemasons, have doggedly discouraged man's ultimate reconciliation with his maker and retarded his salvation. You call it '*Laïcité.*' We call it a tragic apostasy conceived to destroy the good works of our Lord Jesus."

"Laïcité is still widely misunderstood, even in France," Lelouch counters. "Based on two principles, one ethical (freedom of moral conscience), the other legal (separation of Church and state), *Laïcité* highlights the difference between two distinct realities: collective interest and well being, and personal conviction. A democracy cannot survive unless all men are granted, without distinction to class, origin or religious persuasion, the fundamental freedom to choose their poison or antidote, the means to be themselves, to enrich their mind, to be masters of their destiny. Freemasons do not proselytize. We do not preach. We do not sermonize. We do not charge those who do not share our ideals with heresy, we do not threaten them with eternal damnation. That's *your* modus operandi, isn't it?"

Touvier's ashen complexion -- he avoids sunlight like a vampire -- turns red. "We obey the word of God as spoken through his Son Jesus and articulated by Matthew, Mark, Luke, and John, and exalted in Revelation."

"What you obey is an archaic and arbitrary bureaucracy created to abolish freedom of thought and impose obligatory beliefs based on myth and fabrications, not fact," retorts Montvert, who has no patience for people who rely on the Bible to shore up their arguments.

"The evidence that sustains us is Scriptures nourished by faith," Bishop Touvier fires back.

"A faith that ensnares simple souls, that robs them of their judgment and extorts their hard-earned wages. A faith that purports to be doing God's work yet is demonstrably capable of horrific inhumanity. The problem is not that there is no God when things go wrong, but that things go wrong when God becomes part of the equation."

"In the name of decency and fairness, and to help safeguard harmonious relations, I beseech you to reconsider. What good can come from such a premeditated affront?"

"Decency and fairness? You must be joking. As for the Bosch document there was no premeditation, I give you my word," Montvert affirms. "We were informed of an extraordinary discovery and ...."

"You could have kept it to yourselves or quietly consigned it to some obscure art gazette. Instead, you shared it with the Grand Orient and the press, and in so doing you helped set off an avalanche of controversy."

"Talk about safeguarding harmonious relations.... There is no controversy except the one you and *Le Calvaire* are fueling. Let me remind you that we are not handicapped or constrained, like the Church, by a fear of embarrassing facts. Scholarship and history are at stake here, not parochial sensitivities. Freedom of conscience is meaningless without the freedom to express it."

Touvier turns wistful. "What this will lead to is a stain on human dignity, the defeat of trust between people, the triumph of egoism and the loss of emotional tranquility. One can never have true justice, real peace, if God is rejected, if He becomes meaningless, if His teachings are cast aside."

"It takes colossal naïveté or staggering cynicism to

gloss over the rivers of blood that have been spilled in the name of God, that continue to flow as we speak" Albeniz counters angrily.

"Let it go, Bishop Touvier," Montvert offers in a conciliatory tone. "Look on the bright side. The Bosch story is yesterday's news. By tomorrow, no one will remember, no one will care. By year's end, France and the rest of the Christian world will be aglow in Christmas lights. The season will foster feelings of good cheer and lofty resolutions, short-lived as they may be, and life will go on."

"The Church has been grievously injured."

"Only in it pride, not its essence."

"It's a matter of principle."

"How can you talk about principle when you deny man his right to reject ideas that contradict reason?"

"Principle steels me against fear."

"Without fear, man is a *golem*, a robot, a soulless automaton."

Montvert pauses, looks away briefly then, smiling softly, fixes his gaze on Touvier. "Faith may steel you against fear but it doesn't protect you from your past. For you are a relic of the past, a very dark one at that, and against all common sense you refuse to come out of the shadows."

Bishop Touvier falls silent. He understands all too well Montvert's insinuation. He is the grand-nephew of Paul Touvier, a thug and womanizer who, with the support of the Catholic Church and under the command of Klaus Barbie -- the "Butcher of Lyon" -- massacred seven Jewish hostages in a small French village. He later masterminded the execution of 50 French Jews. In 1946, sentenced to death in absentia by the French courts for treason and collusion with the Nazis, Paul Touvier is arrested. He manages to escape, probably with the help of accomplices. In 1966, invoking the 20-year statute of limitations on capital punishment, he applies for a pardon and petitions the court for the restitution of confiscated property. In 1971, French President George Pompidou pardons him, causing a public outcry that escalates when it is revealed that most of the property Touvier claims as his own was stolen from Jews deported to Hitler's death camps. A new arrest warrant is issued in 1981. Eight years later, he is found hiding in a monastery where he had been granted refuge, *"an act of charity toward a homeless man,"* according to the abbot. At his arrest, further evidence shows that he had been protected for years by the Catholic Church in Lyon, and later by members of the Traditionalist Catholic movement. Touvier is also found to have played an instrumental role in the murder of a prominent human rights leader and his wife, and in the deportation of a number of Jews to the East. He is defended by a right-wing monarchist attorney who later becomes president of a Traditionalist Catholic organization. A Traditionalist Catholic priest of the Society of Saint Pius X acts as his spiritual advisor in court. Found guilty, he is sentenced to life imprisonment. In 1996, he dies of prostate cancer at Fresnes Prison near Paris. A Tridentine Requiem Mass is offered for the repose of his soul at a Paris chapel.

•

• •

At midnight, unable to convince Touvier that his bowdlerizing mission is in vain, Lelouch adjourns the meeting and the men part. Lelouch offers to reconvene at a later date for another round of talks but he insists that the Grand Orient shall not be deterred in its quest to serve the interests of scholarship and truth. Bishop Touvier brushes off the invitation.

"There can be no dialogue if the Church's teachings are contested."

"In other words, it's your way or no way," says Montvert.

Touvier casts one last bitter look at Montvert but says nothing.

As the prelate's limousine pulls from the rain-slick curb and fades away swallowed by the fog, Montvert wonders if the bishop might be asking himself whether the blessings of unshakable priestly devotion carry with them the curse of remorse.

He then turns his thoughts to the next project at hand: the translation, annotation and dissemination of Hieronymus Bosch's tell-all manuscripts.

MARXISM OF THE RIGHT

ARCHBISHOP TRENTE-TROIS is livid. Nonplused, overcome by doctrine-driven emotions, Pope Benedict XVI seeks relief in meditation and prayer from the ungodly indifference and iniquity of the secular world. Old hatreds, some encoded, others expediently embraced on the long road to the papacy, submerge him and quell the image of ecumenism he has strived so hard to convey in otherwise hackneyed, sanctimonious public addresses that underscore how woefully out of touch he is with the modern world. For a moment or two, his thoughts turn to the golden age of Church supremacy. The Congregation for the Doctrine of the Faith was still known as the Holy Inquisition. The rabble could be manipulated. Fear, torture and the threat of a roaring and all-consuming pyre in the middle of a public square kept the faithful in check.

Unlike his predecessor, the outwardly affable John Paul II, Benedict XVI can be edgy and petulant, overbearing and smug. Clad in the flamboyant garb of his office, living in unimaginable splendor, breathing the rarefied air of opulence, he believes that the Church's waning influence is the result of declining morals, not its outmoded, intolerant view of human instinct, not the false hopes it peddles or the promises it makes of "eternal salvation" in exchange for the forfeiture of all worldly pleasures. He has little to say about the sordid sex scandals that continue to rock his domain. He feels less than passing shame for the intemperance and crimes of his institution. He expresses no sorrow for the misogyny, the devious homophobia. He feels no guilt for his realm's contempt toward the masses. He does not condemn the entrenched and widespread anti-Semitism among his foot soldiers. He has reached the ethereal summit of his "profession" and the promise of beatification in the afterlife has already imparted him with the trancelike aloofness of a canonized saint. He is preparing for the final voyage, not with humility and compassion but with the poise and absent smile of a mystic high on his own godliness. Behind the smile is the seething fury of a wounded reptile. If he can help it, he will not embark for kingdom come without leaving posterity a taste of his own venom.

•

•   •

In France, a secular nation with a long history of anti-clericalism, the Church does not enjoy the courtesies, perks and dispensations accorded "non-profit" organizations in, say, the United States. Tolerated but neither hyped nor courted, the Church subsists entirely on the generosity of the parishioners, many of whom would rather sleep late on Sunday than attend Mass. Its influence on domestic and foreign affairs is trivial, and its henchmen know better than to worm themselves into

France's political affairs. The French Catholic Church has long reconciled with its marginalized status, if not its irrelevance. The clergy would be the first to admit that no French politician will dare mention God in a campaign speech or parliamentary discourse without risking being pelted with rotten tomatoes, or worse.

It is for these reasons that Archbishop Trente-Trois, mindful that discretion in a fiercely secular state is the better part of valor, and unwilling to inflame the situation, decides to let sleeping dogs lie.

In Rome, filled with apostolic zeal, several members of the Curia urge the Pope to adopt a less obliging stance. One of them, the Most Reverend Salvatore Pacelli, a member of the Congregation for the Doctirne of the Faith and an advisor to Opus Dei, demands that *"the authors of this insurrection -- Jews, communists and Freemasons -- be silenced."* He does not elaborate. The Pope responds to this petition with his trademark saintly smirk.

•

• •

Speaking before his fellow Masons at Gerard Groote Lodge in Rotterdam, a frail Jan van den Haag points at a detail of Hieronymus Bosch's triptych, *The Epiphany*, projected on a screen. The original, as are most of Bosch's paintings, is on display at the Prado Museum in Madrid. The central panel, focus of his lecture, depicts the *Adoration of the Magi*.

"Robed in red, Balthazar kneels in prayer before

Mary and the infant Jesus. Staring in the void, Melchior is at his side. Behind them stands the Moorish king Caspar, flanked by a young assistant. The gifts have been offered. It is in these exquisite works of gold and silversmithing that are revealed subtle and tempting hints. At Mary's feet, placed near Balthazar's helmet, is an intricate gold carving depicting Abraham's aborted sacrifice of his son Isaac. The object is so heavy that it pins down a pair of toads, medieval symbols of heresy.

"Melchior's tunic is adorned with a silver caplet or mantle upon which is reproduced a scene from the Queen of Sheba's visit to King Solomon's palace. Caspar wears a splendid white robe bordered around the collar and sleeves with a delicate lace pattern of acanthus leaves, a bright green southern European plant that inspired the design of the Corinthian column capital. On the hem, winged monsters peck at forbidden fruits. In his hand is a myrrh-filled goblet on which is carved the story of the three heroes offering David water. The jeweled strawberry Caspar holds is also an emblem of heresy.

"The ostensible serenity that the *Adoration* conveys is quickly shattered by the disquieting figures lurking in the manger's shadows. Look carefully, my Brothers. One character in particular, furtive and irresolute, a trancelike emptiness burning in his eyes, is neither naked nor clad, neither barefoot nor shod. His right shoulder and leg are bare, and what appears to be a cable tow is tied about his naked right arm. His eyes seem fixed on a point in space inaccessible to the viewer, perhaps *Ein Sof,* limitless space, time without end."

The assembled Masons look at each other and nod. What is being replayed in this ancient, tell-all picture, graphically and irrefutably, is the reenactment of a Masonic initiation. The Nativity scene, fleetingly the focal point of this troubling painting, is now displaced and trivialized by a rite in which is invoked Further Light -- truth and knowledge -- and which rejects the stagnancy of myth and unbending belief.

What van den Haag suggests, without divulging the origin of his provocative conjectures, is that Bosch could have been familiar with early Masonic lore, thus adding fresh evidence that an embryonic form of Freemasonry existed long before current tradition suggests.

Three days after he regales fellow Freemasons with his titillating presentation, Jan van den Haag, a descendant of Jakob Haymovich who married into the Bosch family in 1685, and a blood descendant of the great artist, dies in his sleep at the age of 83. European lodges send delegates who gather to pay tribute to their fallen Brother at a brief but poignant Masonic funeral. A lambskin apron tied around his waist, white gloves adorning his hands, he is buried at the Jewish cemetery in Rotterdam. Heir to the Dutch throne, William-Alexander, Prince of Orange, delivers the eulogy.

Van den Haag's last will and testament bequeaths the original Bosch document, including the telltale appendices, to his Lodge, Gerard Groote, named after the 14th century worldly educator who believed in linking spirituality with enlightenment based on scholarship and logic. Preaching a life of simple devotion based on early Christian teachings, denouncing the clergy's values and practices as decadent and evil, Groote founded The Brethren of the Common Life. Members of the brotherhood take no vows. They neither solicit alms nor accept them. They aspire to cultivate the "interior life," and they work for their daily bread. Brothers (and Sisters) devote themselves to literature and education. Except for a handful of clerics who had attended the prestigious cathedral schools of Paris and Cologne, there were few scholars in the land, even among the high clergy, most of whom were illiterate. Martin Luther studied under the Brethren of the Common Life at Magdeburg before transferring to the University of Erfurt. His exposure to the Brethren's rational approach to education is said to have sparked the Protestant Reformation.

Gradually, the curricula introduced by Groote's fraternity, rudimentary at first, add courses in the humanities, philosophy and analytical theology.

In his testament, Hieronymus Bosch speaks of the influence Groote had on him.

•

• •

In New York, invited to address Cosmopolitan Lodge, an affiliate of the Grand Orient of France, Montvert warns against the defection, deformation and sharp swing to the right taken by American Freemasonry. Snubbed by most Masonic jurisdictions in the United States, calling it "irregular" or "clandestine" because it does not oblige its members to profess a belief in a *Grand Architect of the Universe* -- "God" -- but welcomes agnostics and atheists in its midst, the Grand Orient is embroiled in a scandal it is powerless or too timid to quell. A renegade group of flag-waving American Masons has obtained, through lies and subterfuge, a patent to represent the Grand Orient of France in the U.S., and to operate as an associate. Little in the otherwise liberal, left-of-center, humanist French fraternity is palatable to the average "red-blooded" American, less yet to the diehard, jingoist, religious fringe that has since hijacked and sabotaged traditional Freemasonry in America and disfigured it by turning a tabernacle of learning and truth into an intellectually sterile refuge for the geriatric set. So the renegade group is playing by its own rules while usurping and basking under the presumed cloak of decorum that Freemasonry confers.

Montvert's talk is entitled, *Personal Thoughts on the Subversion of American Freemasonry -- Then and Now.*

"From its earliest origins," he begins, "Freemasonry has met with political and religious hostility. It has mystified and drawn the ire of the uninitiated. Often unrelenting and violent, antagonism toward Masons has focused on their advocacy of progressive concepts such as Liberty, Equality and Fraternity. Its fiercest enemies also contrived to thwart the spread of key Masonic tenets: free thought, tolerance, the pursuit of truth and the radical separation of Church and State.

"Persecution of Freemasons has always been fiercest in times of social and religious turmoil and during those great upheavals that have led men to war. Such epochs are marked by an absence of "Light," scarred by a pronounced decline in the civilizing effects of reason and traumatized by fits of collective religion-driven madness.

"Most of you should be familiar with the Morgan Affair. Instituted in 1828, the American Anti-Masonic Party was a minor political faction founded in reaction to the mysterious disappearance in 1826 of William Morgan, a disgruntled Freemason who threatened to publish a book in which would be revealed Masonic secrets. Members of his lodge tried to set the publishing house on fire. Morgan was later arrested on charges of petty larceny. Someone paid his debt and covered his bail. He was released from jail and promptly abducted. He allegedly disappeared, never to be seen again. The incident sharpened the dread that the Masons inspired and galvanized the churches to join in a crusade against the rising so-called Jacksonian Democracy (a less than 'democratic' system that extended voting rights to white men only and promulgated 'Manifest Destiny,' the notion that Americans should expand control from the Atlantic to the Pacific at the expense of native populations). Andrew Jackson was a high-ranking Mason who frequently spoke in praise of the fraternity. Another wave of anti-Masonic fury, this time less political than religious in nature and intent, erupted in 1872 and lasted until 1888.

"The Vatican, Hitler, turncoat French General Pétain and Stalin, to name a few, were all rabid foes of Freemasonry. Hitler feared and hated Masons, along with Jews, Gypsies and homosexuals, all of whom he consigned, in the name of eugenics, to concentration camps, gas chambers and crematoria. Nazi Germany considered Freemasonry a tool of international socialism. Communists viewed it as an elitist agent of bourgeois values. The Craft had already been dealt a mortal blow in the 1917 Bolshevik uprising. Fearful that underground lodges might have survived in Russia, Stalin, a schizoid megalomaniac, reinforced the ban on affiliation under penalty of death. Freemasonry disappeared or lay dormant in post-war satellite nations until the collapse of the Soviet Union. It is still frowned on or banned in totalitarian and theocratic societies.

"Enemies of Freemasonry in America, where the Craft has steadily lost its original character and essentially didactic, cultural and social objectives, look to the 1789 French Revolution for evidence of its pernicious influence. After all, they claim, the insurrection was largely inspired and engineered by Freemasons, among them celebrated philosophers such as Voltaire, Montesquieu and Jean-Jacques Rousseau. Tenuous as the link between Freemasonry and anarchy may be, what these critics neglect to say is that, thirteen years earlier, Freemasons had inspired and engineered the American Revolution. No one can argue that both events helped purge an infant America and a tired, corrupt and bankrupt France from the clutches of monarchs, freeloading aristocrats and parasitic clergy.

"Always stranger than fiction, the truth, alas, is no match against deep-rooted biases, malice, lies and ignorance. So the anti-Masonic crusade blazes on in America as well. Fire-and-brimstone evangelical pastors, Catholic priests and self-styled preachers can be heard haranguing against Freemasonry on short-wave radio stations and in houses of worship across the land. Some of the enormities leveled against the fraternity are so outlandish as to discourage rational discourse.

"Lacking hard facts, detractors spin yarns filled with mind-boggling untruths, myths, rumors and innuendoes. It may not be altogether by accident that the vicious attacks they mount and the infamies they spout can be found, almost verbatim, in *The Protocols of the Elders of Zion* and other anti-Semitic and anti-Masonic tracts circulated by the supremacist fringe.

"This year marks an important personal milestone. I celebrate twenty years as a Master Mason. As some of you are aware, during that time, from afar and on regular visits to this continent, I have tried to help re-energize American Freemasonry, to help transform it from an anemic, uninspired sanctuary for old men into a force for world good. I have long been mindful of the conspiracy orchestrated by reactionary elements at Grand Lodges throughout the U.S., and I warned against the ultraconservative mandates that have transformed Blue Lodges into little more than glorified men's clubs.

"This transformation, this mutation which took decades to bear fruit, drove American Freemasonry into irrelevance. It became an anachronism when it ceased to be an instrument for enlightenment and social reform, when it turned inwardly and changed from an alliance of free-thinking, progressive men -- think of George Washington, Paul Revere, Thomas Paine, Benjamin Franklin, among other mavericks -- into a bastion of religious and political conservatism out of tune with Freemasonry's essentially liberal values.

"In essays, lectures and personal communications, I urged American Masons to enrich their intellect, to get involved, to speak out against injustice -- foreign and domestic -- to denounce corruption and political chicanery. And I warned that so long as Freemasonry remained an insular, closed-circuit, self-serving glorified guild rather than a shrine of learning and intellectual refinement, it could never rise above the level of a mundane service organization.

"My words fell on deaf ears. Freemasonry in America is a travesty, as is the mythical image that America has of itself. It makes a mockery of its ancient roots, principles and objectives. There is this bulimic rush to 'create' Masons, whether 'truly qualified' or not, and in direct contravention of the rigorous standards -- ethical and intellectual -- for initiation.

"Worse, as religious fundamentalists continue to malign and defame Freemasonry from without, a group of Freemasons, all of them 'states' rights' advocates and pious Christians who view even benign governance as malignant and deserving obliteration, are now laboring from within to turn what is already an avowed bastion of conservatism into a vector of ultra-right-wing ideology. Their philosophy, if one can call it that, is largely embodied in the canons of 'Libertarianism,' a political movement with an ambiguous name and a deceptive agenda that mirrors Ayn Rand's capitalistic tirades and Jefferson Davis' sophist arguments. Both Rand and Davis are the darlings of neo-conservatives and modern anti-abolitionists. Rand exalted selfishness; she called it a 'virtue.' Davis referred to slavery as that 'peculiar institution' and a 'stepping stone' for the Negro to become 'perfect.' Davis believed that slavery was a *temporary necessity in the development of the cotton trade in the South.* Evidently, suggesting that perfection could only be reached by emulating the white man, the same concept held toward attempts to *civilize* and ultimately exterminate large numbers of Native Americans.

"An aversion for fact isn't merely the habit of a few Internet cranks; it's actually Libertarian doctrine: Any government is bad. Capitalism is noble. Worker activism and unions are evil. The poor are pampered good-for-nothing freeloaders who deserve their fate.

"This radical perspective unites free-market economics with a no-exceptions attachment to private property rights. It has a sham concern for human liberty (except for its own), and it preaches that society should be completely free to develop without any guidance or control from the state, which should be eliminated (except of course where it serves the purposes of Libertarianism).

"It is these rank-and-file Masons, these very disciples of Libertarianism, a form of Marxism of the extreme right, that are now attempting to usurp the good name of Freemasonry to advance political agendas that are not only inimical to democratic ideals but violate every ancient Masonic precept.

"It is no coincidence that Abraham Lincoln said of Libertarians, *'The perfect liberty they seek is the liberty of making slaves of other people.'* Less than a century later, Franklin D. Roosevelt astutely and prophetically added, *'The test of our progress is not whether we add more to the abundance of those who have much; it is whether we provide enough for those who have too little.'*

"In conclusion, my Brothers, I would suggest that Libertarianism is the diametrical opposite of Freemasonry, which believes that the 'state' should benefit society, not just the elite; that it needs to rely on the best that science and history can teach, not legend, blind faith and fiction; and that it must be flexible enough to produce greater freedoms and prosperity for all.

"On all these counts, Libertarianism simply doesn't stack up. Once people are able to be rational about politics, I expect them to toss it out as a practical failure and a moral mess apt to pollute and disfigure Freemasonry."

The talk, the most combative Montvert had ever

delivered, receives less than a lukewarm nod. Perceived as being more anti-American than tactless toward American Freemasonry, it is written off as "unnecessarily antagonistic" even by the Lodge's most moderate Masons.

A visiting Brother, Jeffrey Krieg, Master of the John C. Calhoun Lodge in Charleston, South Carolina, takes Montvert's oration as a personal affront and a threat against neo-conservatism and evangelical Christianity. He challenges Montvert at refreshment.

"You Europeans are all alike. You confuse love of God and country with bigotry, intellectual immaturity, vulgar provincialism and jingoism."

Montvert looks at Krieg. His is the face of the United States he knows. His professional dealings with various museums across the country take him there regularly. He knows America but, after all these years he confesses he is still baffled by it. His bluntness, his outspoken atheism, his urbane, liberal, cosmopolitan, eclectic background have made it difficult for him to get close to people of such vastly dissimilar inclinations. Of America, which forswore all princes and potentates in exchange for the majesty of self-rule, he had long since distilled a flag-waving, God-obsessed nation wallowing in abject promiscuity while clinging to its puritanical past, given to hero-worship and gluttonous consumerism, enthralled by its grandiose self-view and readily seduced by the idolatrous slogans it keeps coining in its own name. Of Americans, he had deduced a sanguine, gregarious and generous people, outwardly cocksure, inwardly skittish, in awe of status symbols, deaf or hostile to exotic ideas, and who, owing differences in temperament, tastes and perceptions, he a restless cynic, would never really get to know. Human nature denatures man. It is the chief impediment to harmony among the species.

"I confuse nothing," Montvert replies. "I observe. I witness the adulteration of traditional Freemasonry and lament its decline into a netherworld of banality in which Masons are mass-produced, not to enrich the world with their erudition and commitment to social causes, but to help sustain a fossilized, intellectually inert organization."

"That's your interpretation, one we do not share. Your little speech tonight was less than constructive and...."

"Freemasons should be free, as they are in France and elsewhere, to advance unconventional positions and discuss contentious issues, especially if they are rooted in truth, without getting bent out of shape."

"Brother Montvert, with all due respect," Krieg whispers, a scowl etched on his face, "you are not in France. Moreover, the truth is a subjective concept rooted not in fact but in perception. Last, it is a time-honored convention among American Masons to leave politics and religion outside the lodge. If the Master had known in advance of your intentions he would have rescinded his invitation or asked you to choose another topic."

"The truth knows no geography. It's not a gut feeling. It can't be negated by intuition. The truth is a self-standing reality, observable, verifiable and, once disclosed, indelible. It is not subject to change. It's a constant: 2+2=4. The square root of 9 is 3. Water is composed of two molecules of hydrogen and one of oxygen. The distance between Earth and the Moon is 240,000 miles. Light travels at 186,000 miles per second. The Earth revolves around the Sun, not vice-versa. I am familiar with your conventions and I believe they contradict the tenets and practices of traditional Freemasonry. And so does the Master of this lodge who, in the interest of free speech and the edification of its members, approved the subject of my talk well in advance."

"Have you considered that your concept of truth, and the manner in which you dish it out with such disdain for other people's feelings, come very close to hatred?"

"Hatred? Listen to the maniacal soul-robbers who harangue their congregations. Look at the transfixed masses of 'born-again' who sway and swing and rock, their arms outstretched toward heaven as they pray for the conversion of the Jews, these 'unfulfilled,' 'incomplete' Christians, these accursed Christ killers. What you have...."

"That's false, and you know it. The Jews and Israel have the full support of Christians."

"Get real. Support of Israel by evangelical groups is a subterfuge. What they really aim at is the dismemberment of the Jewish race and culture. They are fooling no one except those who are ignorant of their diabolical objective. As I was saying, what you have in this tidal wave of religiosity are all the minutiae needed to bureaucratize intolerance for the glory of God. Besides, hatred is not an alien emotion in America, is it? Tell me about the hatred of *injuns* and *redskins,* of *niggers, tar babies* and *alligator bait* and *jigaboos,* hatred of *wops, kikes, hebes, yids* and *hymies, polacks* and *bohunks,* hatred of *camel jockeys* and *ragheads, chinks, japs* and *gooks* and *frogs* and *spics....* What a remarkable ethos for a nation claiming to have been founded in defense of tolerance and in pursuit of justice."

"Your antagonism is alarming." The tips of Krieg's ears glow red.

"No, Brother Krieg, what is alarming is the religious fundamentalists' mission to infiltrate and exploit the coercive power of government. No less frightening, is this movement -- Libertarianism -- seductively labeled to invoke noble principles but which, in truth, is being corrupted by profiteers and political mutineers to conceal an agenda of unfettered capitalism and religious orthodoxy. People who consider themselves Libertarian would cheerfully curtail the liberties of those who disagree with them. Industrialists who dump toxic wastes into rivers and lakes also call themselves Libertarians, as do those who would flood the world with assault weapons because they favor a 'free-market' economy ... but would criminalize stem-cell research, pot-smoking, abortion and same-sex marriage because of their high moral convictions. In the long run, such *laissez-faire* -- or is it an expedient political gambit -- paves the way toward theocratic control. We in Europe, Freemasons and men free from the dogmas that devour the American right, will not let that happen."

Krieg, his right forefinger simulating the barrel of a revolver, pokes at Montvert's chest. He smiles and murmurs, "You're a brave man, Montvert, perhaps too brave for your own good. Good luck."

A POTENT NARCOTIC

O N DECEMBER 15, the Vatican issues a closed-circuit inter-diocesan proclamation challenging the *"absurd allegations of overly-imaginative secular art scholars,"* and accusing them of attempting to *"disparage the Holy See, discredit the Church and demoralize Catholics everywhere."*

The next day, *Le Calvaire* publishes an unsigned editorial affirming that there is no proof that Hieronymus Bosch's paintings were anything but the ingenious creation of an otherwise pious orthodox Christian. The column further asserts that Bosch's patrons were high-ranking members of the nobility and clergy, and that King Philip II of Spain, one of the most conservative Catholic monarchs of his time, acquired a large number of his works. Absent from this baseless claim is the fact that the dour inquisitor-king actually impounded Bosch's most striking works not because he was fond of them but because he feared that the artist mocked royal and papal authority and that some of his succulent creations would arouse "impure" thoughts.

Adopting a didactic tone, the editorial further claims that it is a hyperbole to equate Bosch's interpretation of the world to Surrealism or that his visions can in any way be subjected to Freudian analysis.

"Bosch never read Freud and modern psychoanalysis would have been unintelligible gobbledygook to anyone during the Middle Ages."

Stepping into its own trap, the editorial concedes that

"what we call 'libido' was regarded as original sin by the Church and condemned. Today, what we regard as the expression and influence of the subconscious, the Church in the Middle Ages saw the intervention of God or the Devil. It is possible that modern psychology allows us better to understand the lingering magnetism Bosch's work elicits but it cannot shed any light on their meaning and intent, neither those of the artist himself, nor what his contemporaries thought of it. It is doubtful that psychology can explain the spiritual energy that animated his baffling work."

Then, surrendering to wishful thinking, the opinion piece argues that

"Bosch, it is certain, did not attempt to tamper with his audience's subconscious. He sought instead to impart moral and spiritual verities. This is why his paintings have always had a very precise and deliberate meaning. It is for this reason that one must look for Bosch's sources in religion, in the language and popular rituals of his time. His art reflects, no more, no less, the hopes and insecurities that gripped society at the twilight of the Middle Ages."

Art, by definition, is a proclamation. Artists, by nature and conscious intent, "tamper with their audience's subconscious." They do not "imitate life" to satisfy some reflex for mimicry but to convey an idea, to impart a mood, to stir the senses. Turning litigious in its final stanzas, the editorial cautions against

> "overly enthusiastic academics who skew the results of their investigations so they match their preconceived ideas."

What a remarkable characterization of "revealed" religion.

•

• •

The playful vigor of Colombian artist Fernando Botero's corpulent characters makes Montvert smile. Their heftiness, deadpan expressions and seeming lack of self-consciousness dispel any tendency one might have to mock their mammoth proportions. The phone rings as Montvert admires his new acquisition, a signed lithograph of a foppishly attired dancing couple by the beloved painter.

"Yes?"

"Bishop Touvier."

"What can I do for you?"

"Your obsession with that fifteenth-century dauber is causing needless confusion and unease among Catholics. Assuming the remote possibility that some of his work is caricature or catharsis, satire or criticism -- of what practical value can such disclosures be to modern society, five hundred years after the fact?"

"The pontiff and the village priest keep asking the same question when they are reminded of the cold indifference or cheerful acquiescence of the Church to the slaughter of Jews. Do not expect posterity to be lenient. It has a way of stirring the past."

"You despise Christianity, don't you?"

"Despise? No. But I have news for you. I'm not too fond of your competition either -- Judaism or Islam. I'm wary of any religion not confined to home and house of worship. I panic when it is foisted on society, when it intrudes on personal liberties."

"You must stop maligning us. What harm have we done you? What dark compulsion drives you to slander an institution that obeys God's commands, opens its arms to the perplexed and the poor and the distraught and the forgotten, and tries to spread love and instill hope where there is none?"

Montvert and Touvier have a long, animated conversation about religion. Montvert attempts to draw the bishop in a dialogue steeped in pure reasoning. Touvier clings to doctrine and the rote rehashing of a script that suffers no poetic license, even if the truth is sacrificed in the process. Montvert argues that the underpinnings of religion -- mysticism, the supernatural, blind faith in an invisible but all-knowing entity, the theatrical rituals, the taboos and strident proscriptions -- are all contrived to enslave man, not liberate him. Touvier demurs, arguing that man cannot survive without spiritual guidance and a belief in a higher power. Montvert counters that religion suffocates like a strait-jacket.

"Did you happen to watch Christiane Amanpour's recent investigative report," he asks.

Aired on CNN and rebroadcast several times, the three-part *"God's Warriors: The Clash Between Piety and Politics,"* offers a caustic if sobering overview of the three major religions' susceptibility to intolerance in the service of deity and of their relentless effort to sway or control national politics.

"Yes, I did," Touvier replies without elaboration.

"Surely, you will agree that carried to extremes, religion is a dangerous aberration that renders men insane."

"Isolated fits of violence by deranged individuals must not be allowed to sully the nobility of monotheism, to eclipse its good works."

"Isolated? Nobility? Good works? What Amanpour's cameras captured is the bare face of dogma running amok, Bishop Touvier. This is how organized religion, if allowed, transforms society into a citadel of intolerance, into an incubator for hatred and persecution. Your own history is dripping with examples of sectarian hatred, of pogroms against 'heretics.' It is the contradictory command to love one's enemies while regarding alien or divergent doctrines as subversive and hostile that fuels the conflict."

Montvert, eager to unclog Touvier's selective amnesia, reminds him that more than half a century after the end of the Second World War, revisionists, among them high-ranking members of the French Catholic clergy, stubbornly deny that the Church, whose age-old anti-Semitism harmonized with Germany's objectives, cooperated with the enemy, sometimes even exceeding their demands. He also reminds him that the defeat of Germany, the Vatican had feared, would bring down the conservative systems that form the first line of defense against communism. On the other hand, the Vatican had concluded that a victory by the Allies would lead to France's demise and the end of civilization. This was a nihilistic goal, the Church asserted, to which Jews were committed. This grotesque assessment was turned to profit not only by the unscrupulous, the defeatists and common traitors, such as Touvier's great-uncle, but by rich entrepreneurs who, all else failing, had everything to gain from an alliance with Hitler and the Pope.

"*N'est-ce pas*, Bishop?"

Bishop Touvier is at a loss for words. There is little he can say to contradict Montvert without betraying his indelible prejudices or appearing to be the dismissive, unbending zealot he is. Adopting priestly hauteur, he cries out:

"I feel sorry for you, Montvert. You are causing us grievous harm. Perhaps God will forgive you, perhaps not. Remember: There's no greater truth than God. Adieu."

Montvert wonders whether the bishop is conceding defeat or telegraphing a veiled warning. Not one to dither, he snaps, "You've got it all wrong, Bishop. There's no greater God than truth. Good day."

•

•   •

Montvert is annoyed. There's so much he could have said to Touvier to make his case, or at least to nettle him. But a tirade risked corrupting the truth, debasing valid arguments and cheapening the sorrow that overwhelms him when memories rush in. Anticipating an eventual war of words, he had pulled and set aside several documents from his files -- labeled "Weapons of Mass Vexation" -- but he never got a chance to use them.

One was a banner headline in the New York Post quoting the late John Cardinal O'Connor's bombastic declaration that *"God is a man"* -- meaning a male, not a female. How this otherwise moderate prelate had reached this anatomical conclusion remains a mystery. Another was a copy of a letter by O'Connor's spokesman, Father Whalen, to a friend, a journalist and fellow Freemason, which reads,

> "His Eminence has asked me to inform you that he has no time to comment on the issues addressed in your article."

The article, also submitted to the Rev. Billy Graham, and similarly snubbed, chronicled the assassination of streets children in Central America by agents of the state. Busy telling the poor to "go forth and multiply" and preaching against the use of condoms, the Church has yet to denounce this ongoing daily wave of social cleansing.

Another story, Montvert's favorite, underscores the

psychotic nature of religion. Datelined Rome, February 11, 2008, it reads:

> "The 150th anniversary of the appartions in Lourdes of the Virgin Mary was marked in Rome by a procession that culminated at St. Peter's Basilica, Christianiaty's most hallowed edifice, where a rib of Bernadette Soubirou, revered by the Church and blessed by the Pope as a saintly relic, was placed on display before an adoring crowd of worshippers."

A rib! A macabre artifact idolized not in the remote Australian outback, the depths of darkest Africa, the jungles of Papua New Guinea or the Peruvian altiplano, but in a nation where the Rennaissance was born, where the wholesome breezes of Enlightenment helped air out the stench of ignorance and superstition.

"Ghoulish. Idolatrous buffooneery," Montvert had grumbled.

Suspended midway between waning faith and reason, Manuel Albeniz had once wistfully suggested that "people seem to need religion. They think society would collapse without it." Coming to his senses, Albeniz had quickly added, "Of course, the more hocus-pocus and histrionics religion delivers, the more plausible and persuasive its doctrines become."

Montvert had agreed with his friend. The grand spectacle of religious rituals, the necromantic melodrama of the Mass, the boisterous exuberance of evangelical "revivals" all enthrall the faithful and they keep coming back for more. But he had rejected the notion that humans *"need"* religion or that some apocalyptic meltdown would ensue without it.

"Religion is a catechism in which are cast in stone proscriptions and commands, threats and penalties enforced with incantations and theatrics that the faithful are enjoined to regard as essential to their life and well being," Montvert had added. "Faith is a potent narcotic but only those who have been 'turned on' (generally by force from infancy) succumb to its lethal 'high.' People are not born naturally predisposed to believe in fairy tales. Nor do they innately acquire an 'addictive personality.' One does not become a junkie until one has sampled and presumably become 'hooked' on the toxic merchandise. Religious belief is not the product of evolutionary instinct and very rarely a conscious choice. It is first infused in an unsullied psyche then reinforced through repetition and the discipline of fear."

Nor would mankind wander in a spiritual desert without 'divine' guidance. Morality predates religion by millennia. Cultural anthropologists have shown that even the most "primitive" societies maintain codes of behavior that are not religious in origin, scope or intent. Conversely, history has demonstrated time and again that vast quantities of blood were shed in the name of "God" and that it continues to be spilled in modern sectarian conflicts. In contrast, no war was ever waged to advance the cause of atheism.

Montvert had been brought up in an ambiance utterly devoid of religious affectations. An absence of ceremonial spirituality at home did not create a void in his life and, as he tells anyone willing to listen, he found the notion of an omnipotent, ineffable, unknowable creator/judge/destroyer preposterous even as a child. (He had learned how to deny being a Jew in half a dozen languages during the German-occupation). Yes, he had gone through his "mystical period," immersing himself in the study of Zen, the Tao, Tantric Buddhism, Hinduism, Shinto. Like his father before him, he had spent countless hours "meandering in stupefied fascination" through the Kabbalah's cerebral minefields. At first, he had felt intellectually challenged but the leaps of comprehension, not to mention the leaps of faith the Kabbalah demands, had left him exhausted and confused. Ultimately, it was the Kabbalah's hyper-deterministic character that had prompted his father to dismiss this, the most arcane of all Jewish philosophical systems as *"a disquieting pastime for the idle, borderline monomaniacs or candidates for lunacy."* The Kabbalah, he would conclude, not only trivializes human hopes, knowledge, dreams and the legitimacy of voluntary action or inaction, it effectively discourages rational and deliberate action of any kind. Any system that pledges to temper human perplexities and lead to enlightenment through occultism, he held, delivers false hope and leads to disillusionment.

It was shortly after his father's death, troubled by his stormy apostasy and anxious to jettison some of his own dismissive preconceptions that he ventured for the first time in the Kabbalah's arcane realm. Enthralled and bewildered at first, often driven to mental exhaustion, he too eventually tired of its multilayered circularity, flagrant contradictions and maddening esotericism. He was not being ushered into some liberating "beyond." Rather, he was being shoved and jostled and inveigled to probe the "nothingness" that dwells within. He found such mental pirouettes more taxing than he had imagined. Thought can travel no farther than its point of origin. The mind cannot fathom itself. Faced with the imponderable -- the very essence of Kabbalah -- he bowed out, humbled by the magnificence of paradox. His brief but intense foray into Kabbalah would not be in vain. Careful, measured readings yielded fresh insights on the depth of Jewish thought. He would later marvel at the magnitude of its influence on the works of Mirandola, Spinoza, Leibniz, Swedenborg, Kafka, Borges, Benjamin and Derrida. He would also discover that the root of Kabbalistic doctrine had been enunciated, much earlier and in considerably simpler language, in the Tao and Buddhist teachings. No matter the originality of a concept -- *"There is nothing new under the sun"* (Ecclesiastes, 1.9) -- he admitted that he too had been transformed, however imperceptibly, by the Kabbalah's awesome, wrenching mental exactions. But Montvert's excursions into mysticism were inspired by an unquenchable thirst for knowledge, not a need to take refuge in some ideological sanctuary.

"I think, therefore I doubt," he had exclaimed at last when he awoke from a blinding sleep and shed the last vestiges of forbearance for senseless beliefs. Nine-tenths of his family had perished in Hitler's gas chambers and the "inscrutability of God's designs," at best an offensive rationale, had since become loathsome.

He rebuffed the notion that man is born sullied by some "primal offense," that pain ennobles the soul and that sentient beings need to be ruled by an arbitrary system of faith-based values and protocols.

In religion's imaginary goodness, he discovered not a path to enlightenment but an instrument of deceit and emotional enslavement. The transformation from fence-straddler to mutineer was gradual, filled with misgivings. At first, he found religion's mystique inscrutable. He had meandered through its occluded allegories and bizarre canons like an explorer in a strange, uncharted wasteland. He had glimpsed the very faint light that religion claims to shed but found only vast and gloomy shadows. It is in the shadows that his senses, now accustomed to the darkness, caught sight of a glow, a radiant luminosity that rinsed his pupils free of the gritty debris of credulity. He now understood that blind faith, not truth; prejudice and fear, not common sense, threaten humankind and consign it to bondage.

Like others before him, he had absent-mindedly tolerated sundry propositions and viewpoints along the way, some of which he even peddled, parrot-like, out of stupidity or intellectual sloth, not for the intrinsic virtues with which they were purportedly endowed.

Assembly-line rearing, fashionable in the days of his youth, had instilled a value system that seemed strange if not utterly without merit. He had been coached by otherwise doting parents to defer to authority with robot-like reverence: Applaud politely but do not innovate. Respect your elders. Venerate your teachers. Salute your superiors. Obey the boss. Comply with representatives of the public order. In short, he was to idolize or at least yield to all species of adults of dubious pedigree who had by now forgotten what it feels like to look at a very menacing world from three feet off the ground.

In school, he had been programmed by coldhearted masters to smile or fight back the tears, to subdue, sometimes to smother very raw feelings under the pretext that such perfunctory bearing is what society expects of a good little boy and later, of a *mensch*. Precocious and sly, he knew he was not and could never be a good little boy. Nor did he aspire to *menschhood*, a status not clearly defined or imagined at the time. But he understood that pretending to do what others anticipate -- feigning religion, simulating approval of orthodox concepts, conforming to time-honored trends -- can bring on small rewards or, at the very least, shield one from censure, reprimand or retribution -- all of which he eventually incurred when he tired of pretending and transitioned at last from conciliation and irresolution to defiance.

Later, as his peripheral vision improved and his depth perception deepened, he began to ask questions, the very questions he now regretted not asking Bishop Touvier:

Why are we susceptible to pain and defenseless against the fury of disasters -- natural and manmade -- that, religion insists, are wrought against us "for mysterious reasons" by some capricious supernatural force?

Who is this "maker" who inflicts (or tolerates)

atrocities for "the good that comes from them"? What cunning and irreducible absolute orchestrates without apparent aim -- or turns a blind eye to -- the paroxysms that convulse his realm?

What "intelligent designer" remains stone-silent while the sobs of his creation are never heard?

What "ineffable" entity is this, whose ear is inattentive and whose breast is unfaithful to the throngs who call on him and seek his succor?

What cruel despot decrees that his subjects will parrot words not their own, that they will blindly obey the injunctions of self-anointed envoys, tremble at their threats and admonitions, mouth off supplications and jeremiads and recite guilt-ridden prayers of indebtedness and veneration, all repeated *ad nauseum*, day after day, to a God who never shows his face, never bares his heart, never sheds a tear, never says he's sorry, a God who grants life and, with it, the fear of death?

The questions, mulled over when he was still a child, were in fact declaratory statements conjugated in the interrogative. This he believed: Religion is divisive, repressive, irrational and detrimental to the pursuit of harmony among men. It belongs, if at all, in houses of worship or at home. It has no place in the bedroom, schools and government, much less in the crafting of a national psyche.

"Karl Marx was right," he had told Touvier in response to some exasperating platitude. "Religion is the opiate of the people. But unlike opium, which puts users in a state of blissful lethargy, religion inflames passions and brings the worst in man. The sectarian hatreds and paroxysms of ferocious religiosity that convulse the planet epitomize religion's toxic character. "

Eventually, Montvert had concluded that "God" is a useless and costly hypothesis with which he could dispense. And crypto-agnosticism turned into overt atheism.

•

• •

But Touvier, the consummate obfuscator, would have resorted to parable in order to prop up an indefensible hypothesis. He would have developed a scenario based on an irrational argument, supported a premise with another premise.

"Ten starving children come to your door begging for a morsel of food," he would have sermonized. *"But you have barely enough to feed one. What do you do? God can't be everywhere. He can't right every wrong, heal every wound, redress every injustice, punish every sin."* Touvier would have then shrugged his shoulders, arched his eyebrows with saintly fatalism and hoped that his twisted supposition, like some eloquent and impregnable court summation, would silence the prosecution and help exonerate a scoundrel.

Unruffled, Montvert would have hacked through Touvier's Gordian Knot by feeding one child and hypnotizing the other nine into believing that they had feasted on a five-course meal. This would have underscored the nature of God's unpredictability, the randomness of his heartless neutrality. It would also have added weight to Montvert's assertion that children do not challenge the "realities" that parents, teachers and "spiritual" shepherds promote.

"We learn soon enough," he would have added, "that the fairies and the monsters that inhabit our worst childhood nightmares are impostors. Yet, with sufficient parental guidance, including crafty counsel not to wander beyond the limits of the "realities" that parents peddle, and punctuated by the constant drumbeat of religious indoctrination, children enter adulthood fully conditioned to believe -- and keep alive -- charades that owe their stubborn longevity to blind faith."

Sigmund Freud may or may not have analyzed Bosch's paintings but it was he who postulated the now widely accepted concept that we are the product of our subconscious. He was careful to add that the "subconscious" is not an amorphous and indelible entity. The subconscious is the end-product of many dynamics, the least of which is genetic. Our subconscious is molded, fashioned and often perverted by early childhood experiences and through encoding (the planting of fixed ideas) by parents, educators, clergy and other figures of authority. No one is "born" a believer or an atheist. No one comes out of the womb a Democrat or a Republican, a fascist or a Maoist. Serial killers and good Samaritans are made not sired. The subconscious is an easy prey. It can be hounded, abducted, duped. It can be dragged to the altar of paganism and idolatry (worship of statues), forced to engage in cannibalism (Communion) and, as a bonus, pushed toward terminal psychosis (the belief in life after death).

In the philosophy of religion, Occam's razor is sometimes applied to argue the existence or non-existence of God. While Occam's razor does not attempt to disprove God's existence, it offers a compelling argument: in the absence of convincing proof that such entity exists, disbelief should be preferred. Montvert rejected the suggestion that Occam's razor compares apples and oranges. Instead, he maintained, it illustrates, with blinding clarity, that while, say, Christianity has branched into often dissimilar and almost always bickering factions -- each cheekily claiming exclusive access to God -- atheism, by its very axiomatic simplicity and absence of pretense, has never changed. A lack of belief cannot be codified. There are no Orthodox, Conservative or Reform atheists. All atheists speak in a single voice. No ideological rift can splinter them.

Nor do atheists feel compelled to defend their ideas as are religious people fixated on convincing others of the validity (and "divine origin") of their beliefs. An atheist is quite content not to believe; a believer is consumed with the need to nourish his belief and the urge to "share the glad tidings."

Atheism has no catechism. It warns against the tyranny of absolutist ideas, not hell and eternal damnation. It promises no redemption other than freedom from absurd and useless beliefs and crippling guilt. It dispenses no indulgences or exemptions from sin in exchange for bribes; it has no pontiff and no "church," no crimson-attired "princes" who live in Babylonian splendor, no avaricious plate-passing beadles; it delivers no sermons, it proffers no threats of fire and brimstone, it promises no agony- or bliss-filled afterlife. Atheists do not maintain an Index of Prohibited Books. They don't burn books. They have no need for a Congregation for the Doctrine of the Faith which, by its very existence, attests to the perilous fragility of religion. Atheists refuse to drift along a stream which is not of their own choosing and are eager to puncture all alibis invented by human beings to spare themselves from being accountable for their choices. Atheists, seldom spontaneously but after much internal turmoil and self-inquiry, conclude that there is no God and that, therefore, human beings are neither created nor pervaded by anyone or anything that can have a plan or idea of what they will be like before they come into being, or before they develop by their own free action. Atheism is simple, clear, unequivocal.

Religion clings to fictions that do not exist in the absolute vacuum of pure thought, but must be "planted" in the mind to burgeon, i.e.,

> "God" is the source of all essence and reality; Jesus was the son of "God"; he was born of 'immaculate' birth; he rose from the dead and his death and rebirth open a portal to eternal life."

Whoever or whatever he was, Jesus opposed formal religion, abhorred the mix of politics and worship, and held the self-aggrandizing bluster of virtuous believers in contempt. Religion is learned, not intrinsic. An addict needs his fix because he indulges in drugs in the first place. One does not "get" religion except through osmosis. People never exposed to religion will not suddenly develop an urge to embrace outlandish beliefs without the intervention of some powerful and persuasive medium -- a renunciation of life's sweetest gifts or an irreversible psychotic episode. Religion may have "tamed" some people but it has poisoned the soul of many others and led to intolerance and lunacy.

We're all born with a blank slate and only parental rearing, the environment and societal pressures mold us into cookie-cutter replicas of our would-be retrofitters. We're all endowed with a brain capable of discerning the truth but the brain is soon so badly mangled by indoctrination and rote repetition that we submit to a ritualistic, synchronous reflexive behavior that we are enjoined to believe benefits us and "society."

Yes, we are the stuff that stars are made of. We are a product of eons of fusion. But "fusion" implies only the amalgamation and compacting of disparate elements. Man's parts are infinitely larger and more diverse than his whole and it is the parts that result in geniuses and idiots, assassins and philanthropists, captains of industry and social parasites, adventurers, human dynamos and couch potatoes, loving parents and infanticides, great artists and uninspired oafs.

It is all that, and more, Montvert is convinced, that Hieronymus Bosch tells us in his always stunning, forever unsettling commentaries on the human condition. The great master belongs to the world. His message to posterity, Montvert insists, will not, must not be silenced.

CARDINAL SINS

CAREFUL SCRUTINY of a number of paintings by Hieronymus Bosch offers strong circumstantial evidence that he may have belonged to a proto-Masonic lodge. In *The Marriage at Cana,* on display at the Boymans van Beuningen Museum in Rotterdam, can be found several esoteric allusions, some Kabbalistic in origin, others eerily reminiscent of Masonic symbolism and ritual. Two events seem to be taking place independently. In the background, behind two pillars -- Boaz and Jachin -- is an altar composed of twelve superimposed cubes. A magician, perhaps a master of ceremony, points to the second cube from the top tier. In the foreground, twelve guests are seated at an L-shaped table. Standing, his back turned, a child hails the group. His left hand is extended upward, the space between thumb and forefinger forming a ninety-degree angle, his right clasping a chalice. A knotted sash encircles his left shoulder.

At first glance, the scene is reminiscent of Christian liturgy -- bread, jugs, a statuette of St. Christopher hunched under the weight of the world, the pelican, symbolic of Jesus -- all conspicuously poised on the altar. A plausible interpretation, one supported by a number of scholars, including Montvert, suggests that the banquet celebrates the marriage of the Jew Jacob of Almaengien, then-Master of the Brotherhood of Free Thought. Almaengien, who had sponsored Bosch in the execution of his most hermetic works, is also known to have been an active member of the Brotherhood of Notre Dame, to which Bosch also belonged. It is reasonable to assume that Bosch may in turn have had some contact with the Brotherhood of Free Thought.

A troubling and as yet unsolved enigma centers on the swan which, along with the boar's head, is being served to the guests. It is known that 14th century mystics considered the swan a symbol of debauchery. An old Flemish proverb -- white outside, black inside -- alludes to hypocrisy, an inference further supported by the presence on the swan's flank of a crescent moon, then the emblem of heresy (and, to some, a symbol of homosexuality). Yet, the dark meat of the swan was a prized delicacy at the time and a staple dish at the Brotherhood of Notre Dame's frequent feasts, including the one organized to celebrate Bosch's own initiation.

Another intriguing detail involves the numerical placement of various objects on the three tiers above the altar: seven on the lowest, five on the middle one and three on the topmost. Three, five and seven are the numbers of steps on a winding stairway that an Apprentice must climb to have revealed to him the secrets and obligations associated with the second degree of Masonry, or Fellowcraft.

The most conjectural clue of all is a mannerism common to all the banquet participants, guests and servers alike. Their open hands, curiously in full view, form a near-perfect right angle -- a square, one of the tools used by operative masons and, symbolically, by speculative Masons, in their labors.

The eternal conflict between good and evil, vice and virtue, damnation and redemption is rarely as forcefully allegorized as in The Temptation of St. Anthony, on exhibit at the Museu Nacional de Arte Antigua in Lisbon. The triptych reeks with malevolence: here a flight of winged monsters, demons, reptiles and witches, there the ordeal of fire, the whole forming a kind of merry-go-round of horrors calculated to bewilder and torment St. Anthony in his quest, after untold trials and self-denials, for spiritual peace.

The left panel, the most relevant in Masonic terms, focuses on a small wooden bridge extending across a frozen pond upon which an exhausted St. Anthony, supported by two Brothers, continues his penitential sojourn. A third helper, a "friend" or guide, long identified as one of several *"à la Hitchcock"* Bosch auto-portraits, offers, along with his bare left knee, yet another hint of the painter's initiation into the secret rites. Most striking is the crushing fatigue endured by the group. Despite the assistance given him, St. Anthony seems to have given up. He is overcome with a stifling loneliness, another stage in his perilous journey, made all the more unbearable in that grandest of all voyages -- life -- by despair and faithlessness. Only his guide's eyes are open. Perhaps only he sees the way while a demon-bird, an escutcheon representing a geometer's square embroidered on his tunic, taunts a corpulent priest who gets rich dispensing indulgences to incorrigible sinners.

●

● ●

What is Freemasonry? The question is best answered by
affirming what it is *not*. It is *not* a secret society, a
religion, a satanic conclave devoted to the anti-Christ.
This, the world's oldest and largest fraternal
organization, the most misunderstood, reviled and feared
union of men (and women) who seek enlightenment and
dedicate their lives to its dissemination, has no designs or
influence on world banking. It is not laboring to bring
about a New World Order in which -- depending on
one's leanings or baseless "evidence" -- mankind is either
consigned to slavery in the service of capitalism or
delivered into the clutches of communism. Freemasonry
advocates no sectarian faith or practice. It seeks no
converts. It does not solicit members. It raises no money
for faith-based institutions, at least not in Europe. It has
no dogma or theology. In many lodges it is forbidden to
discuss religious (or political) issues. It offers no
sacrament and does not claim to bring about spiritual
salvation. Despite demented allegations by individuals
who have never seen the inside of a lodge, Freemasons
do not embrace a new religion, much less an anti-
Christian one, any more than they would by joining a
political party or a community service organization.
There is nothing in Freemasonry that opposes religion
except when it meddles in politics. It accepts men and
women of all faiths who believe in freedom of
conscience, subscribe to democratic values and universal
human rights, and embrace the principles of Free-

masonry. Candidates must be free of prejudice and dogma, and willing to commit to a lifelong quest for the truth through study, introspection and altruism. Candidates to Freemasonry are not subject to religious rites of passage. They are sometimes asked if they believe in a "supreme being," but their concept of "deity" need not coincide with the Judeo-Christian model. Freemasonry respects all faiths but it does not engage in theology.

The rudiments of Freemasonry began to meld into a coherent but as yet unstructured concept sometime in the 15th century. It slowly acquired its modern character in the mid-1500s or early 1600s. This was a period of great political turmoil and religious intolerance. Freethinkers, among them agnostics and atheists, and men who wanted to endow God with less paranormal features, were unable to meet and exchange ideas without arousing suspicion, sparking arguments and risking persecution. Masonic lodges soon became temples of rational discourse, inquiry and erudition where men from all walks of life joined to explore new ideas. While the fraternity has maintained its original character and objectives in Western Europe, with Grand Orient Freemasonry being the most secular, free-thinking and radical, it underwent a gradual and significant trans-formation in the U.S. Grand lodges and their constituents steadfastly refused to get involved, to speak out against injustice, corruption and political chicanery. The fraternity turned inwardly, becoming an insular, closed circuit and self-serving institution. It dramatically lowered or abolished heretofore high standards for admission -- among them free thought, tolerance and intellectual refinement. It turned populist, veered sharply toward the political right, made a belief in deity mandatory. It draped itself in the flag instead of embracing a holistic worldview. It became a haven for mediocre men seduced by titles, regalia, medals, certificates, citations, ribbons, plaques and other accolades very rarely bestowed outside of the U.S. except to reward extraordinary service to society.

If there is a link between the waning eminence of American Freemasonry and a decline in membership, it is perhaps because, after having been initiated, new Brothers in America are left suspended in a vacuum. They've paid their dues. They've become small cogs in a large machine busy keeping its own wheels turning, a sort of Rube Goldberg perpetual motion contraption out of sync with its own driving force and, in the long run, utterly without purpose other than self-perpetuation. The intellectual nourishment, spiritual stimulation, social and philosophical dimensions so vital to Freemasonry, are nowhere to be found. American Freemasons are content to bask in the brilliance of a star-studded Masonic constellation: George Washington, Ben Franklin, John Hancock, Paul Revere, Lafayette, Mozart, Bolivar, Garibaldi, Jonathan Swift, Goethe, the Roosevelts, Truman, etc.... They look up to these men as though their wisdom, creative genius and courage are transferable through some generational osmosis. They are not. If a child should not bear the burden of his ancestors' misdeeds, nor should he revel in his father's fame. He must seek his own paths of glory. The above-named

Brothers were men of action, builders, shakers, movers, gadflies, thinkers and creative geniuses long before they knocked at the outer door of a lodge. It is they who enriched Freemasonry -- not the other way around. They all believed in a better tomorrow, a more just, progressive and nobler human society. All were inspired by other thinkers and revolutionaries. American Freemasons believe the revolution is over. It's not. So long as there is injustice and suffering, ignorance and intolerance the spiritual revolution must go on. It is this and more that Michel Montvert must have tried to convey during his visit to Cosmopolitan Lodge in New York, and for which he was so harshly censured.

•

• •

By decree, and following unanimous approval by its constituent lodges, the Grand Lodge of Honduras invites Dr. Manuel Albeniz to Tegucigalpa to confer him with honorary membership for his

> "dedication to the promotion of the arts, for his unwavering labors on behalf of Freemasonry and for his unstinting espousal and defense of Truth and Reason."

The conferral is held at the Francisco Morazán Lodge, named after the martyred Central American statesman and Freemason. A public reception in his honor is later held at the Maya Hotel in the capital's upscale Colonia

Palmira.

In an interview with *Diario Tiempo*, Albeniz hails the tardy "national reconciliation" that appears to have healed a country long exploited by U.S. economic colonialism and further traumatized by U.S-engineered coups and "dirty wars." He knows that *reconciliation* is a euphemism, a pact rammed down the people's throat that has eviscerated an entire society. He knows that the U.S.-trained military thugs who committed atrocities in the name of "national security" were decorated, pardoned and their victims forgotten. He knows that mass graves were covered with fresh topsoil and generals and colonels were absolved and are now living in serene retirement, some of them in the U.S. He knows that this mock *reconciliation* whitewashed torture, mass murders and disappearances, that it exonerated the criminals and coerced the victims' families to "forgive and forget" while denying them any compensation.

Albeniz is less ambassadorial in an off-the record comment on the Honduran Church's coziness with that nation's military establishment, a tryst he characterizes as contrary to Christian ethics. Careful not to name names, Albeniz also criticizes high-ranking prelates who, "owing indifference, personal inclination or stratagem," shield known pedophile priests from imminent prosecution and reassign them to remote parishes in the wilds of Honduras. News of the recent assassination of a Maya tribal counselor, the fiftieth in less than ten years, inspires an icy denunciation by Albeniz of the "state-sponsored cleansing" of ethnic minorities by ranchers and land speculators.

A day later, Albeniz is found dead, face down in a remote corner of the vast municipal garbage dump outside Tegucigalpa, felled execution-style by a bullet to the back of his head. Overhead, vultures glide in wide sweeping circles, surveying life and espying death, smelling it as it wafts from the bottomless chasms and sulfurous pits where the corpses of street children are often dumped. Emboldened by some irresistible effluvia, a few make landfall. Waddling from side to side, wary and cunning, they fight for the foulest scrap of offal in their path.

A police account, endorsed by a press all too eager to bamboozle the public with fabrications rather than risk the authorities' wrath by reporting the truth, concludes that Albeniz wandered "in an unsafe part of town where he was robbed and killed by 'delinquents'." Eyewitness reports that men driving a late-model SUV with dark-tinted windows dumped the lifeless body are ignored.

Spain's envoy to Honduras calls for an investigation. Back-room diplomacy triumphs when the papal nuncio in Madrid intercedes, first with King Juan Carlos I, then with Prime Minister José Luis Rodríguez Zapatero, urging them to discourage Honduras from pursuing the matter "in the spirit of appeasement." Hondurans need not be coaxed to look the other way. They have a long history of sloth and indifference. A slapdash inquest by a jaded constabulary drowns in a sea of apathy, ineptitude and obscurantist bureaucracy, and the murder, one in a daily cavalcade of homicides, is quickly forgotten.

Insisting that the case be kept from going cold, the Spanish ambassador in Honduras is recalled to Madrid and hastily replaced. Rumors that men working as gofers for right-wing Cardinal Oscar Andrés Rodríguez murdered Albeniz are promptly muted when it is learned that the alleged perpetrators are in fact members of an undercover squad headed by Police Chief Ofelia Galeano, commander of Honduras' Anti-Narcotrafficking Detail. Galeano is later charged with soliciting bribes from high-level drug traffickers and conspiring, with the help of a number of U.S. Drug Enforcement Agency operatives, to siphon large sums of money from fines assessed against criminals. Galeano, a devout Catholic, quietly resigns her police post and is promoted to a low-profile but high-power executive position in the Honduran National Congress.

•

• •

When Padre Antonio Quetglas, vicar of Tegucigalpa's Archdiocese, blamed the investigation of parish priest Enrique Vásquez Vargas, a self-confessed child molester, on a *"worldwide Jewish conspiracy to deflect attention from Israeli atrocities against Palestinians,"* was he speaking his mind or echoing the voice of his master, Cardinal Oscar Andres Rodríguez? Or were the unceasingly fanned embers of anti-Semitism being stirred yet again by the Church to deflect from another sex scandal? The cardinal, a fast-rising star in the Roman Catholic hierarchy who was scolded by the Anti-Defamation League for voicing anti-Jewish sentiments -- and summarily forgiven -- put Reverend Vásquez to work in two remote Honduran parishes. He also shielded Vásquez, who had spent time at two "clergy treatment centers" and has since become an international fugitive, from prosecution. Claiming he'd rather *"go to jail than harm one of my priests,"* Cardinal Rodríguez steadfastly kept the police at bay. The 44-year-old Vásquez, who fled his native Costa Rica in 1998, served in at least two U.S. dioceses before absconding to Honduras where he was arrested in 2007.

Cardinal Rodríguez, once short-listed for the papacy, first drew fire in the U.S. in 2003 when he characterized the media covering the scandal as *"protagonists of a persecution against the Church."* Speaking on condition of anonymity -- "I don't wish to be 'accidentally' hit by a bus or have my Coke laced with strychnine... -- an eminent Honduran journalist offered this laconic perspective:

"Cardinal Rodriguez is ambitious and arrogant. He hobnobs with the rich and famous. He disdains the poor. His sermons are more political than pastoral and his private conversations are peppered with an-Semitic remarks."

The rich and famous include the political elite, members of Opus Dei and high-ranking military officers, many of whom committed atrocities during the "dirty war" of the 80s. While three incorruptible archbishops were murdered, two in Guatemala, the third in El Salvador, for blowing the whistle on human rights violators, Rodríguez maintained a cozy association with caudillos and generals. He continues to coddle the plutocrats and the military and still hopes to occupy the papal throne in the not too-distant future.

●

● ●

Manuel Albeniz's remains are flown to Barcelona. Officers of the Grand Lodge of Spain conduct a Masonic funeral in his honor and memory. The Museo del Prado in Madrid flies the flag at half-mast. He is cremated and his ashes are scattered over the ruins of an old Jewish cemetery. Jewish graves in Spain, some going as far back as the 12th century, are slowly being emptied and the bones reburied in unmarked plots. A more sinister form of inquisition now endeavors to erase all memory of a once thriving and influential Jewish presence in Spain. Long gone is the Iberia of the "learned" King Alfonso X of Castile (1221-1284) who surrounded himself with Jews, notably in his great scientific, cultural and commercial enterprises.

●

● ●

On January 21, 2009 Pope Benedict XVI, reaching out to the extreme right-wing of the Catholic Church, invalidates the excommunication of four schismatic bishops, including one whose denial of the Holocaust provokes outrage. The revocation is seen as a clear sign that Benedict's four-year-old papacy is increasingly supporting traditionalists hostile to the sweeping reforms of the Second Vatican Council, which sought to create a more modern and open Church. Among the men reinstated is Richard Williamson, a British-born cleric who, a week earlier, had said in an interview:

> "I believe that the historical evidence is hugely against six million having been deliberately gassed in gas chambers as a deliberate policy of Adolf Hitler ... I believe there were no gas chambers."

Williamson was elaborating on a speech he had made 20 years earlier at Notre-Dame-de-Lourdes church in Sherbrooke, Québec:

> "There was not one Jew killed in the gas chambers. It was all lies, lies, lies. The Jews created the Holocaust so we would prostrate ourselves on our knees before them and approve of their new State of Israel ... Jews made up the Holocaust, Protestants get their orders from the devil, and the Vatican has sold its soul to liberalism."

Like Williamson, the other four reinstated men were members of the Society of St. Pius X, founded by French Archbishop Marcel Lefebvre in 1970 to protest the modernizing reforms of Vatican II. Archbishop Lefebvre made the men bishops in unsanctioned consecrations in Switzerland in 1988, prompting the immediate excommunication of all five by Pope John Paul II.

In a letter sent to followers, Bishop Bernard Fellay, director of the Society of St. Pius said,

"Thanks to this gesture, Catholics attached to tradition throughout the world will no longer be unjustly stigmatized and condemned for having kept the faith of their fathers."

Somehow, a tradition that inhibits religious freedom and promotes anti-Semitism does not seem to enhance Church unity or improve its reputation. But in recent years, Benedict has made other concessions to Lefebvre's followers. He allowed a broader recitation of the Tridentine rite, a service that was made optional in the 1960s and which includes a prayer calling for the mass conversion of Jews.

•

• •

Pope Benedict arrives in Israel on May 11, 2009. Ill at ease and diffident, the pontiff speaks like a historian, like someone observing a not-so-distant past from the secure sidelines of officialdom. It is clear that the horrors to which he alludes with professorial aloofness have little more than academic significance. He fails to mention the Nazis by name, to characterize their actions as cold-blooded murder. He glosses over his own past so he doesn't have to explain it.

A Papal spokesman defends Benedict:

"He can't mention everything every time he speaks."

It is this abject spin doctoring that prompts demands for a few extra words by the Pope about the details that haunt his Papacy, about the fact that of all the people on earth it was a man with his background who was chosen to be Pope.

Hanoch Daum writes in his column.

> "You were not asked to do something unprecedented or heroic. All that was required from you was a brief, authoritative and compassionate sentence. All you had to do was to express regret. That's all we wanted to hear."

Another editorial called the visit *"a missed opportunity."*

> "[His] statements condemning anti-Semitism and Holocaust denial lost their potency because of his lukewarm remarks at Yad Vashem [Holocaust Memorial]. The Pope's visit shows that there is no real dialogue between Israel and the Vatican."

While the Pope's past as a member of the Hitler Youth and the German Army was widely acknowledged, it is understandably very difficult for some people to get beyond it. What revolts Michel Montvert, who lost nearly nine-tenths of his family to Hitler's gas chambers, is that cardinals of the Catholic Church, meeting in secret conclave in the Sistine Chapel, knowing these facts and aware of the Church's dubious history during the Second World War, chose among all the candidates in their midst to select the man who would later call himself Benedict.

This was blindness or arrogance or worse. Certainly, they knew their choice would unsettle at least one group of people sharing a long and difficult history with the Church. Certainly, they might have foreseen a moment when the new Pope would stand before a Holocaust memorial and be seen both as a representative of his Church and of his past. Yet, they went ahead, as if by design, and appointed as the head of an empire with the Vatican's discreditable history someone with a blemished history like that of former Cardinal Joseph Ratzinger. He could have, Montvert observed, easily addressed these issues in the state whose creation was in part a by-product of that abomination. The Vatican's argument that he had addressed them before was unconvincing because by choosing not to do so in the one place where such a statement of acknowledgement and regret would have made the most difference, he raised questions not about a choice but about the motives behind it.

●

● ●

It is impossible to assess Pope Benedict XVI's ostensible love of Jews based on a homily he delivered fifteen years or so ago, or on his assertion that Catholic-Jewish relations remain his "top priority." A preoccupation with interfaith harmony suggests the existence of an underlying conflict. For the Catholic Church, the 20th century opened with a strong conservative reaction against a modernism that infused life into the moribund institution. The chief instigator of this reaction was the

Sacred Congregation for the Doctrine of the Faith, which tells Catholics what they may and may not read and defends against any form of heterodoxy.

As John Paul II lay dying, Catholics prayed for a Third World pope. But the old, diehard, Eurocentric Vatican insiders picked a German so the Church could retain its stranglehold on power instead of dealing with real-world issues like poverty, overpopulation, AIDS and priestly buggerism.

In effect, the Inquisition was reinforced under Cardinal Joseph Ratzinger. The doctrinaire prelate was summoned to Rome to cover and redress the perceived theological failings of John Paul II. Ratzinger was promptly appointed Prefect of the Congregation and immediately launched a conservative rear-guard assault against the progressive faction of the Church, especially in Latin America, and with the assistance of Opus Dei, the Vatican's most radical right-wing (and anti-Semitic) crusaders.

Ratzinger was quick to enunciate the theoretical basis of the Mass which, in his view, was being diluted by "Liberation Theology," the oxygen-rich ministry that redefined and enlivened Catholicism south of the Rio Grande. Under Ratzinger's guidance, the political, anti-Socialist aspect of the Inquisition was beefed up. Two of his acolytes, Cardinals Sebastian Biaggio and Bernardin Gatin (both members of Opus Dei) led a silent campaign that resulted in the "defrocking" of scores of bishops and parish priests whose greatest sins were to teach poor children how to read and write, and encourage workers to unionize.

Short on political clout but long on memory, the poor in Latin America have not forgotten that Pope John Paul II paid a courtesy call on then-president of El Salvador, Armando Calderón Sol -- a man widely suspected of engineering the assassination of Archbishop Romero and, with Ronald Reagan's backing, of masterminding the massacre of 900 men, women and children at El Mozote by U.S.-trained death squads. Surely the Pope must have known that in El Salvador, like elsewhere in Central America, the rich and powerful have systematically defrauded the poor and denied most of the people any voice in the affairs of their country.

The election of Benedict XVI has reopened old wounds. Though in decline in Latin America, the Church maintains a deeply symbiotic rapport with the plutocracy and keeps tapping into the reactionary power base to maintain both doctrinal monopoly and political custody over the masses. This has in large part contributed to the success of a shrill and militant form of evangelical Protestantism marketed in theater-like arenas by skillful actor-preachers who drive their congregations to fits of trancelike religious fervor dangerously reminiscent of hysteria.

•

• •

Eleven days after the Pope's visit to Israel, the incoming and retiring Archbishops of Westminster launch a joint offensive against atheists and secular society. At the installation of the Most Reverend Vincent Nichols at

Westminster Cathedral, his predecessor, Cardinal Cormac Murphy-O'Connor describes a lack of faith as "the greatest of evils." Surrendering to hyperbole, he blames atheism for war and destruction, implying that it is an even greater evil than sin itself. While the hostility that atheists occasionally voice toward religion is limited to words, -- no war has ever been waged in the name of atheism -- Murphy-O'Connor speaks of the "battles that will be won and lost in the effort to sustain a Christian presence in secular society

"The things that [result from secularism] are an affront to human dignity, destruction of trust between peoples, the rule of egoism and the loss of peace. One can never have true justice, true peace, if God becomes meaningless to the people."

Archbishop Nichols, glitteringly vested in newly minted gold miter and chasuble, and sounding more like a warrior than a man of God, declares open season against what he calls the "secular agenda."

But angry reaction to flippant comments Nichols makes about child molestation casts a shadow over the installation. Referring without a hint of apology to a report that exposes decades of abuse by Catholic priests and nuns in Ireland, he warns that the scandal threatens to overshadow the "good done by the religious orders."

Michèle Elliott, chief executive of the charity Kidscape, is indignant.

"This is ludicrous. He should have issued a

straightforward *mea culpa*. This is all about the children; the rest of them be damned."

Patrick Walsh, a spokesman for the group Irish Survivors of Child Abuse, also condemns Nichols' remarks.

"Rubbish is too kind a word for what the Archbishop has said. He ought to take a long hard look at the character of the people he is talking about and ask himself if they are capable of being good."

Tom Williams, of Oxford, sums up the proceedings with beguiling irreverence and wit. He suggests that the words of Murphy-O'Connor and Nichols would not be out of place in a Monty Python farce.

"Have two supposedly intelligent men ever spouted such nonsense? God bless the atheists -- oh, how we need them to protect us from these nitwits."

THE INVENTOR SPEAKS

**The Appendices of Hieronymus Bosch,
translated from the Flemish and prefaced by
Jan Van den Haag,
with commentaries by Michel Montvert**

COPIED, COUNTERFEITED and cloned but unrivaled, Hieronymus Bosch soars above his imitators. The attention he devotes to the hidden source of things, to the ideals they impart, his contempt for the mighty clergy and for the evils they commit, their intolerance, political dogmatism and theological rigidity, all attest to his nonconformist genius. Also betrayed in his work are the inner paroxysm of doubt and the disgust for his fellow men that must have guided his brush.

His universe reeks of the infernal odor of sulfur. One can imagine the nausea he must have felt as he detailed an orgy of transgressions and elaborate punishments before a public all too familiar with their terrifying realism. The Hell that awaits sinners is not much different from the actuality that punctuates their existence, an actuality they magnify as imagination, fear and the fetters of religious indoctrination subdue and defeat them.

Bosch's prime objective is to communicate with and,

176

in so doing, to respond to a public evenly split between those who will not see, no matter how clearly the truth is expressed, and those desperately thirsting for the freedom to exhume it from an ossuary brimming with myths and lies.

Those who describe Bosch's metaphorical universe as little more than a hodgepodge of devils and monsters simply don't appreciate his creative independence, scathing irony and keen understanding of the social, religious and psychological dimensions of his time and place. The same parochial attitude would later greet the work of modern Surrealists, among them Max Ernst, Paul Klee, Joan Miró, Salvador Dali, and Marcel Duchamps. Bosch does not attempt to stage a utopia. His is a vision of a world not given to meditation and self-inquiry, but consumed with paralyzing dread, most of it the legacy of religious fanaticism, and incessant brainwashing. As such, Bosch's paintings must be seen as docudramas on evil, as "reality shows" so painful in their evocation that it is likely he was not only a witness but a casualty of the horrors he so cunningly recreated.

Alchemy, anticlericalism, human bestiality, death, the cosmos and the apocalypse are the key devices through which Bosch expresses his pessimism about man. Defined as the science beyond the realm of human comprehension, alchemy may have helped him hint at, without leaving incriminating clues, certain aspects of his life, possibly his sexual preferences. Androgyny, the state of being distinguishably neither male nor female, is a recurring theme in his work, with sub-themes -- hollow trees, broken empty eggshells, lots of buttocks and bizarre but unambiguous scenes of sodomy -- create an uncommon link between art and auto-psychoanalysis. His *Garden of Earthly Delights* must be seen as a sexual reverie, a melancholy rumination on the transience of carnal pleasure and the brevity of life.

Bosch's anticlerical zeal often borders on blasphemy. His most celebrated paintings, *The Haywain, The Ship of Fools, The Conjurer,* are rife with caustic denunciations of clerical sleaze -- lasciviousness, malice, cruelty and simony (the buying and selling of church offices). The repressive power of the Church is aggressively flagged in his blazing scenes of Hell. Though it offers no clear evidence of atheism, his work is indisputably anti-religious.

One of Bosch's sources is the Apocalypse, written by St. John at Patmos and composed of seven visions which suggest that the doomsday literature of the second and first centuries BCE contained essential elements of Judeo-Christian esoterica. Apocalyptic dreams and syncretism (the fusion of different forms of belief and practice) play a significant role in Bosch's tormented cryptographic universe. Obsessed with the prophecies of the End of Days or of the Millennium which, after the fall of the Antichrist, must precede the Last Judgment, Bosch anticipates a Second Coming, not of religious fervor but of intellectual freedom and enlightenment.

A feature of cryptographic art is the use of "moralizing" glances at a Hell we can now deem absurd but which Bosch's contemporaries viewed as real and inescapable. But in attacking the sadism of demons and otherworldly monstrosities, Bosch explicitly condemns oppression, the ghoulish cruelty of man, the ferocity and lust of the clergy and, with caustic wit, even the blatant consequences of anti-Semitism, then already in full swing. Every thief, every blasphemer, every heretic, every evil-doer must be a Jew. Bosch deciphers in the behavior of his contemporaries the absurd authority, the pessimism, the anguish, and the hopelessness that poison their lives.

Magnificent inventor of a cosmos in which the improbable and the inevitable coexist in perilous proximity, Bosch urges us, with cynicism and compassion, refinement and candor, to meditate on the follies of the world. His Appendices, which follow, add uncanny realism and immediacy to a world not so very different from our own. **Jan Henryk van den Haag (JHVH)** ∴

I

"Know Thyself" is an ancient aphorism that encapsulates an indefinable ideal: Understanding human thought and behavior. To understand one's self is to come to terms with others as well, sometimes with less sympathy and forbearance, sometimes with more. Man, however, can never fully comprehend the human spirit because it is quite impossible for him to know himself. The mind can ponder all but its own workings The old Chinese dictum may refer to a less ambitious ideal -- acknowledging one's own habits, temperament, vices, summoning the ability to control them and other aspects of behavior that we struggle with in our daily lives.

In a narrower sense, "Know Thyself" may attempt to point to a question that everyone has asked: What is the meaning of life? To know one's self involves a deeply personal transformation aimed at analyzing one's own perception of reality.

We all defy mortality according to our nature. Some toil without respite to serve others, on battlefields and fields of grain and palace kitchens and slave ships. Others indulge in mind-numbing diversions. Others yet labor to make a statement, to leave a record of their brief passage on Earth. What we articulate through the printed word, in music, carved out of stone, set on canvas, speaks volumes about our inner-selves. Inevitably, such endeavors also reflect an image of the vast universe our eyes, minds and souls are called upon to observe, grasp and interpret.

The world my eyes have seen is the same world of courage and cowardice, generosity and greed, tolerance and fanaticism, honesty and hypocrisy, cruelty and compassion, birth, death, rebirth and the resurrection of ideas pondered by those who came before me but so rendered as to mirror the forms and realities of my time. I have invented nothing that does not already exist in outward appearance or in the nightmares that visit us when scruples, doubts and forebodings haunt our nights.

I, Jeroen Van Aken, better known as Hieronymus Bosch, offer no apology for my optic. What remains unsaid in my modest output, or what onlookers fail to deduce from it, is clarified in the records that follow, each dedicated to a work which I affirm to be entirely my own, executed in my workshop from preparatory sketch to final brushstroke. I have endeavored in each and every case, sometimes with discretion, often with transparent abandon, to protest the scourges that putrefy not only the flesh but the soul of men: the tyranny of inflexible beliefs, irrationality, self-righteousness, deceit and the abominations perpetrated on the simpleminded, the meek and the voiceless by the powerful, whether they be attired in ermine or purple vestments embroidered with gold.

What I call *The Cure of Folly* -- others may choose to call it something else -- is about madness, not the kind brought on by an excess or deficiency in any of the four humors -- black bile, yellow bile, phlegm and blood -- or by bad air, but by the idiocy that affects half-wits who can be tricked to swallow the preposterous ideas of charlatans who peddle instant wisdom and absolution, spiritual salvation and life beyond the grave. Who but those dedicated to our enslavement would have us believe in Original Sin, in Heaven and Hell, in the divine rights of kings, in the infallibility of the Church, and in the immortality of an unreadable soul that ceases to be the instant of our demise? The only remedy against such folly is reason, a faculty with which we are all born and which we must at all times guard against the despotism of tyrants, whether crowned or ordained, and against the oppression of absolute ideas. **H. B.**

Notes

The Cure of Folly is quintessential Bosch. See the "surgeon" who removes the "stone of folly" from a vacant-eyed patient as a nun, a book of medicine balanced on her head, and a pensive witness seem to be meditating on the limits of human stupidity. Worn by the quack, the funnel, a ridiculous headgear symbolizing vacuity and madness; the flower-like "tumor" pulled out of the patient's skull; the dagger piercing his moneybag; the gallows rising in the distance -- all are part of the allusive language Bosch uses to ridicule senseless beliefs and degenerate customs, to mock mass credulity and the vanity of healers who are little more than charlatans armed with lancets and magic potions, leeches, emetics and often deadly purgatives.

Medical knowledge in Bosch's time seems to have stood still. It was steeped in superstition and the Roman Catholic Church dictated the evolution and direction of the healing arts. Any perspective that differed from established Church dogma was viewed as heresy and severely punished. When the Church insisted that illness was the result of trespasses against God, few were in a position to argue. People at the time of the Black Death were convinced they had sinned. Others blamed the Jews for the spread of the plague. Thousands paid with their lives for this calumny.

While physicians believed that "humors" or a surfeit of blood in the body was a major cause of disease, their diagnoses were often influenced by astrology. Medical charts cautioned "surgeons" against certain procedures based on the patient's sign. For example, a person born under the sign Aries could not undergo incisions to the head. One can reasonably assume that the cretin submitting to the "excision of madness" is not an Aries. On permanent display at the Museo del Prado in Madrid, Bosch's celebrated spoof makes one last overarching statement: everyone is insane who surrenders to convention, diktat and ritual. Only knowledge, tolerance and charity can help free humanity from the bondage of ignorance, fanaticism and insensitivity. **M. M.**∴

II

Ingenuity, nimbleness and tempo turn the most implausible sleight of hand into a convincing reality. The same attributes, in the hands of soul robbers and dream merchants, help spread anxiety, fear and guilt-ridden convictions among otherwise lucid individuals. It is this transformation, cunning, swift and irrevocable, that my painting, *The Conjurer*, attempts to represent.

The idea was quite simple. Take a magician, a simpleton gaping uncomprehendingly at the trickery unfolding before him as his purse is being snatched by a thief whose eyes are turned heavenward, and a group of onlookers gloating at the dupe's astonishment. Overshadowed by the adults towering over him, a young boy finds amusement in the larceny. Surging from behind, seemingly out of place, visibly troubled by the proceedings, an interloper stares with dismay at the vulgar deception. I am that intruder; I painted myself into the scene, the better to expose the charlatan who toys with the gullible fools. **H. B.**

Notes

Nothing was known about the origins or gist of this painting, now hanging at the Municipal Museum in Saint-Germain-en-Laye, outside Paris, until the appearance and translation of Bosch's appendices. A meditation on the immorality of proselytism, using an archaic language that resonates with modern vigor, *The Conjurer* or *The Swindler*, as I prefer to call it, alludes with biting irony to the con-artistry of a Church seeking to snare the lost and the gullible into its ever-tightening net. It is yet another chapter in the annals of human stupidity, aptly illustrating the proverb, "he who is seduced by artifice loses his money, and even children laugh at him." **M. M.**∴.

III

What I try to warn against in *The Haywain*, a grand spectacle of a world gone mad, are the deranged mystical premonitions of my time and the horrors they engender. The world is a haystack: everyone plucks from it what he can get. The result is a free-for-all of ambition, envy, greed, hedonism, predation and cruelty. I have no cause to believe that man, little better than beast, will ever change. **H. B.**

Notes

The "free-for-all" is so out of control that it leads many to slip and die under the wheels of the cart while an obese monk, drink in hand, observes the butchery with saintly detachment as nuns hurriedly stuff clumps of hay into hempen sacks.

The Haywain, on view at the Museo del Prado in

Madrid (with a copy at the San Lorenzo Monastery in Escurial) is a graphic satire on the fleeting nature of life, egoism and cupidity. It also warns against the evil of deceitful characters, whether monarch or spiritual guide. It is when the outer panels of the triptych are closed, revealing *The Vagabond* or *Wanderer*, that Bosch's message about decadence most subtly typifies the mentality of the 15th century, a time when metaphysics began to express a pronounced antipathy toward the Church.

The landscape adds to the feeling of impermanence; the narrowness of the path; the rounded hills, the mottled green and yellow terrain. Is this drifter a mad pilgrim, the twenty-second major arcane of the Tarot? Or, as his bare knee suggests, is he an initiate into the occult sciences who witnesses and takes part in life's vicissitudes? It is impossible to tell what his vacant eyes see or where his steps take him as he ventures across a small, unsteady bridge. A dog growls at him. Black birds hover over human bones. Behind him, scenes of brutality and absurdity unfold -- on the left, a murder, on the right a man and a woman dance to the sounds of a bagpipe, a symbol of lechery. Further up, gallows rise on the hill and a gleeful throng gathers to watch a hanging.

The weariness branded on this lost vagrant's features is heightened by a sadness born of regret and irresolution. His is the lot of man torn between the lure of self-emancipation and worry-free conformity. **M. M.∴**

IV

Commissioned by the Brotherhood of Free Thought, and far from being a sermon against eroticism as some of my peers have suggested, *The Garden of Earthly Delights* is the daydream, the open-eyed reverie of humankind as it anxiously, sometimes frantically, attempts to free itself from the oppressive dictates of its worldly lords and spiritual masters. The uninhibited ecstasy I impart in some of my subjects is offset by the reticence, the look of doubt, stupefaction and disenchantment of those around them. Pleasure is fleeting, but only through it can man experience a rebirth of the innocence he enjoyed before his soul was usurped by the merchants of myth and false hope. Regardless of what posterity chooses to say about this work, let it be regarded and remembered as nothing more or less than a satirical comment on the preposterous claim that mankind is tainted by "Original Sin," or that codified rules of behavior and synthetic beliefs can help expunge it. **H. B.**

Notes

There is little doubt that Bosch was a member of a "heretical" sect known as the Adamites, or Brotherhood of Free Thought, a radical group active in western Germany and the Netherlands which strove for a form of spirituality immune from sin, a concept they considered a fabrication and a stratagem for subjugation. Nor is there any doubt that *The Garden of Earthly Delights*, Bosch's most captivating and hermetic work, was commissioned for non-devotional purposes. His characters seem to be cavorting in a setting of exquisite yet alien exoticism, in harmony with unearthly beasts and unfamiliar flora and stirred by a sexuality that takes them to heretofore unknown heights of anticipation and bliss. While artists in Bosch's time painted not for their own pleasure but to meet the crass demands of survival, it can now be argued that an all-consuming wave of anti-clericalism, fed by daily manifestations of papal and priestly misbehavior, and bolstered by a quest for self-knowledge, nurtured Bosch's petulance. A handful of Bosch scholars, for reasons unknown, reject this thesis, now confirmed in the artist's own hand, and conjecture about his art more feverishly than about any other artist. They keep struggling with his fantastical images, choosing to regard them as enigmatic representations of esoteric knowledge lost to history rather than clever metaphors. Yes, Bosch uses every symbolic device available to him. While he lived at a time when the beliefs of the Medieval Church held absolute moral authority, he robustly and steadfastly spoke against them.

There is a strong possibility that certain elements of this painting may have been inspired by the most significant and mind-altering event of his day -- Bosch was forty-two years old at the time -- the "discovery" of America. The left and center panels are drenched in tropical and oceanic atmosphere, evocative of Columbus who, approaching terra firma, thought that the place he had found at the mouth of the Orinoco River was the site of the Earthly Paradise. (Columbus would wax poetic about every new island, beachhead and verdant valley he set his eyes upon). The year when this triptych was created, circa 1492-93, was a time of adventure and discovery, when tales and trophies from the New World sparked the imagination of poets, painters and writers. Although the painting exudes many unearthly and implausible creatures, Bosch's images and cultural references appealed to an elite humanist and aristocratic audience. The conquest of Africa and the East provided both wonder and terror to European intellectuals, as it led to the conclusion that Eden could never have been an actual geographic locale. The travel literature of the fifteenth century is referenced in the imprecise or exaggerated animal forms given life in *The Garden of Earthly Delights*.

The charting and occupation of this new world confirmed the existence of regions previously only idealized in the mind's eye of artists and poets. At the same time, the existence of a Biblical paradise, marketed along with a Purgatory and Hell by the Church, began to be questioned by thinkers and relegated to the realms of mythology. In response, treatment of Paradise in literature, poetry and art shifted toward a self-consciously fictional Utopian imagery that would be further exploited by the religious merchants of false hope.

Art historian Erwin Panofsky admits that,

"In spite of all the ingenious, erudite and in part extremely useful research devoted to the task of 'decoding' Hieronymus Bosch, I cannot help feeling that the real secret of his magnificent nightmares and daydreams has still to be disclosed. We have bored a few holes through the door of the locked room; but somehow we do not seem to have discovered the key."

The "key" to Bosch's universe is in full view and accessible to anyone capable of discarding embedded beliefs and willing to step beyond the allegories into a wasteland where only the truth blooms. **M. M.**∴

V

If I conclude this unavoidably superficial account with *The Prodigal Son*, I do so not because it is my last major work but because it summarizes my outlook on life and on the choices it forces us to make. Embodied in the hesitant posture and bewildered expression of this wretched vagabond, this drifter gray before his time, whose unfocused gaze reflects sorrow and indifference, is the eternal struggle between instinct, purpose and groundless convictions. He must choose between virtue (knowledge) and vice (ignorance). With its crooked, decaying roof, broken windows and shutters, and laundry hanging from the transom, the White Swan Inn, a jug impaled on its gable, offers a picture of immorality that tempts and threatens to hold him back. His steps lead him to the entrance of a bountiful field of grain. At the very moment when he is about to pass through the gate, he turns his eyes away from it. With a hand trembling with indecision, he points to the right path. Will he follow it and gain freedom? Or will he succumb to the suffocating forces of unreason? Disenchantment, suffering, he tells us, is universal and indiscriminate. It begins at birth for both man and beast. It is the duel between his repudiation of an unalterable fate, of a fixed and inevitable future -- and his concept of the world as a godless and irrational affair of ceaseless striving and affliction -- that leads him to shake the last remnants of religiosity. The journey is arduous, the course littered with hazards. It is a one-way voyage at the end of which, he will learn, freedom awaits. **H. B.**

Notes

Serene pastoral beauty and a feeling of foreboding converge in *The Prodigal Son,* on display at the Boymans van Beuningen Museum in Rotterdam, to produce an amalgam of conflicting emotions. A late work with a profane theme, it breaks away from Bosch's iconographic tradition which would have found this conflicted individual either in the arms of a harlot or kneeling penitently in rapt trance. Bosch has chosen this instant frozen in time to remind us that decisions, choices and priorities punctuate and often interfere with the business of living. There are no angels or demons here, no winged redeemers or clawing fiends. The dilemma is created by life in its perceived reality. But the human soul is frail. Brimming with contradictions, irresolute and on edge, he meanders in a world drowning in ignorance and super-stition. Bosch's cynicism is mitigated by pity for man who can find no moral home within himself without freedom of conscience. He stands at the threshold of a door that leads to free will. The significance and message of this work is that it does not find man frozen in prayer, as his contemporaries do, but struggling with his inner self. He lays bare the contradictions of his age, Careful not to judge or indict, his work is an outward meditation on melancholy, on the sadness of the soul, on the frailty of the human spirit. It is also a reaffirmation that life is a protracted struggle toward self-liberation.

A fugitive from conformity and rigid beliefs, Hieronymus Bosch has erected a monument dedicated to the disintegration of all absolutes. The mortar that keeps it standing and defiant was tempered in the crucible of his cosmic vision. In his lifelong search to extract secrets rooted in the subconscious, Bosch cleared the way for artists, writers and philosophers who braved untold obstacles as they sought intellectual independence through knowledge and enlightenment. More broadly, Bosch cautioned society against the slogans, formulas and rote conventions that give life a semblance of symmetry and numbing simplicity. **M. M.**∴.

THE MONKEY AND THE FOWL

O N JUNE 7, 2009 Trinity Sunday, Michel Montvert submits Bosch's apologia, appendices and accompanying annotations to the editor of the *Travaux du Grand Orient*, where they are published a week later. Dedicated to *"Brother Manuel Albeniz, martyred at the altar of dogma and political expediency,"* the controversial document is reprinted in the prestigious Proceedings of the International Academy of Arts. Excerpts are showcased in an article penned by Montvert, *The Trowel and the Cross -- Art and Heresy at the Dawn of Enlightenment*. Bosch's testament is also reprinted in *Secret Architectures*, a scholarly Masonic publication circulated worldwide.

Predictably, *Le Calvaire* fights back. Alleging that a *"an anti-Christian cabal"* is at the root of *"this latest expedition into the distant past by imaginative counterfeiters,"* the unsigned editorial blames *"the subversive forces of secularism, abetted by Marxists, Israelites and Freemasons for this latest assault on the good name of the Church."*

The rhetoric sounds oddly familiar. Montvert swears he's heard that sequence of words before. Then he remembers. Bishop Touvier. But in print, his words take on an ominous hue. This is not the spur-of-the-moment outburst of an angry man set afire in the heat of debate.

The enshrinement of platitudes in the pages of an influential ecclesiastical publication, Montvert concludes, hints at a new phase in the war of ideas. Is he being warned? Threatened?

•

• •

On July 8, on the eve of a global economic summit in Italy, Pope Benedict XVI lashes out at capitalism, calling it, *"nearsighted and short on ethics."* The pontiff is right. The history of human society is the history of class struggle and capitalism, the offspring of greed, wholly dependent on the exploitation of the masses for the enrichment of a few. But His Holiness says nothing about the myopia of religion or the immense wealth the Vatican has amassed over the centuries, much of it the spoils of wars -- at least nine Crusades and the Holy Inquisition -- and booty siphoned off during the Second World War.

•

• •

On July 14, on the 220th anniversary of the French Revolution, Jacques Lelouch, Grand Master of the Grand Orient of France, speaks to the nation. His address, a history lesson for the ages, is broadcast as is custom on French TV, aired on radio and carried by the leading dailies. Championing the cause of secularism, Lelouch reminds his fellow Frenchmen of the events that took the country from serfdom to democracy and he uses the occasion to throw a well timed jab at Bishop Touvier and at the Catholic Church, an institution that maligned and persecuted Freemasons for three hundred years. He gallantly refrains from naming the bishop. He is less gracious with the Church. France's largely secular society openly delights in his irreverence.

"A widely circulated caricature dated 1787, two years before the storming of the Bastille, shows a monkey -- the king -- asking the fowl in the yard (the people) in what sauce they would like to be cooked.

"Another famous French pre-revolutionary political cartoon depicts a rakish nobleman and a smiling, overfed cleric riding on the back of an old, exhausted peasant. The metaphor, concise and painfully real, may have inspired French philosopher and encyclopedist, Denis Diderot, who wrote, *"Superstition is more harmful than atheism,"* to exclaim, uncharitably but to the delight of many Frenchmen, *"Man will never be free until the last king is strangled with the entrails of the last priest."*

"This was the twilight of the 18th century, the dawning of Enlightenment, and France was tired of the ancient and traditional order in which the king is commander in chief, judge, jury and executioner, and Frenchmen were wary of a system that called for the nobility to defend the nation with its sword, the clergy to pray for victory while engaging in political intrigue and cavorting with women of ill repute, and the rabble to toil and pay merciless taxes until they dropped. The king's power was absolute, limitless and issued from God himself. But this king -- Louis XVI -- was an inept military strategist. His officers had lapsed into mediocrity and the Church, fat and venal, made a mockery of religion. The clergy paid no taxes but charged tolls on behalf of the crown, took their cut, and sold indulgences and first-class passage to paradise, with much of the gold they collected diverted and adding to the personal fortunes of many princes of the Church. The commoners -- peasants and bourgeois alike -- crushed by unfair and exorbitant levies, were fuming. Soon, they would open the shutters wide, lean out their windows and shout, *'We're mad as hell and we won't take it anymore....'*

"Talking about the French Revolution, informally but factually and rationally, and without resorting to trendy banalities, is a daunting and humbling task. It's made all the more difficult by the sheer complexity of this event, the contradictory or falsified accounts of its origins, the role of assorted players and by the myths, half-truths and distracting anecdotes that have since entered public consciousness. For these reasons, and given my own views on the subject, this talk will be neither exhaustive nor entirely dispassionate. In the interest of time and decorum, I will focus on the root causes of this history-altering affair -- which I consider more signifi-cant than the incidents that marked it. Owing the gravity of recent happenings, I will unavoidably veer off my prepared statement, not to take needless detours, but to call attention to these troubling distractions.

"About a month ago, in response to a series of widely circulated documents detailing the secret life and provocative work of a legendary artist, and in anticipation of this yearly communication by the Grand Orient, a man unable to subdue his passions but cloaking himself in anonymity, told an untruth in the press. He alleged without a shred of verifiable evidence that Jews and Freemasons are plotting to sully the reputation of the Catholic Church. On this day of remembrance, he would have you believe that the French Revolution, to which we owe our enduring civil liberties, among them freedom of conscience and expression, and the radical separation of Church and State, was an outrage masterminded by Jewish financiers, Freemasons, degenerate philosophers and *other irreligious libertines*. It was not, as every clear-headed Frenchman knows. Nor was the regrettable violence that followed the storming of the Bastille a grotesque act of barbarism against Christian values, as this fellow citizen asserts. Yes, many innocent heads rolled during the two–year frenzy that followed. Alas, this same fellow-citizen, in defiance of fact and against all reason, denies that the uprising was an outburst of irrepressible rage against centuries of misery and oppression. Nor can he countenance the notion that the Revolution lifted the yoke of feudalism from the bone-wearied backs of France's serfs and vassals, or that it helped rid France of a dissolute and manipulative clergy. It is easy to label as murder the beheading of two royal idlers who bankrupted France while they wined, dined, gambled, gathered in prayer, made war, partied and cheered their dogs on helpless foxes. It takes infinitely more courage and integrity to concede that revolution is a process, not an isolated occurrence and, in the case of France, that it was the culmination of a trend whose seeds -- the burgeoning concepts of Liberty, Equality, Fraternity, universal suffrage and the abolition of absolute monarchy -- had been sown long before the conflagration.

"A century earlier, in a letter to Louis XIV, François Fénelon, the king's almoner and a writer well known to French school children, wrote:

'Sire: For thirty years your ministers have violated all the ancient laws in the state so as to enhance your power. They have increased your revenues and your expenditures to the infinite and impoverished all of France for the sake of your luxury at court. They have made your name odious. Meanwhile, your people are starving. Sedition is spreading and you are reduced to either letting it spread unpunished or resorting to massacring the people that you have driven to desperation.'

"A sharp critic of the monarchy, Fénelon was dismissed by the king for uttering truths the king did not want to hear. A hundred years later, under the ham-fisted reign of Louis XVI, the long simmering embers of poverty and despair set fire to the Revolution. Two centuries later, George Orwell defined freedom as *'the right to tell people what they don't want to hear.'* History has a habit of repeating itself when the truth is recklessly ignored -- or distorted by the minions of reactionary ideology.

"Now, this fellow citizen's contempt for Christian denominations other than his own assumes subtler hues when it comes to Jews. His brand of anti-Semitism is abstruse and furtive, tempered no doubt by an agonizing reality: Anti-Semitism is no longer as politically correct as it was, say, during the Inquisition, the Dreyfus Affair or at the height of the German occupation, when his family applauded the Nazi onslaught, wined and dined the enemy and cheered on Hitler's Final Solution.

"His antipathy toward Jews, encoded and tenacious, predates him. The Dreyfus Affair, which dragged for nearly ten years, aroused passions and prejudices that divided France and very nearly triggered a civil war. An epic of treachery, intimidation, fraud, and injustice, it revived and widened the philosophical rifts that polarize the French in times of unrest and discontent: the right against the left, the aristocracy against the proletariat, the clerical elite against the secular masses, anti-Semites against liberals and freethinkers, the Church against Freemasons. The same antithetical ideologies polarized the French during the Revolution, the German occupation and the wars of Algeria and Indochina.

"The 'Affair,' as it is still referred to, began as a banal case of espionage during which French Army Captain Alfred Dreyfus, a Jew, was arrested on the flimsiest evidence, which included forged documents, found guilty by a collusive kangaroo court and condemned to deportation and life imprisonment in a 'fortified compound,' a sinister euphemism for the hell hole that Devil's Island would prove to be. Dreyfus was publicly stripped of his rank and his saber broken in half as crowds shrieked *'Death to Jews! Death to the traitor!'* After enduring five years of incarceration in one of the world's most infamous penal colonies, Captain Dreyfus was first pardoned, thanks to the tireless efforts of Emile Zola. The Supreme Court later exonerated him.

"Dreyfus, who attended Zola's emtombment at the Pantheon, was shot and slightly wounded by a French journalist, a royalist and a pious Catholic whose acquittal following a hasty trial added to the public bile. Unmoved by a growing wave of repugnance sweeping France, most politicians continued to insinuate that Dreyfus was guilty, or they aligned themselves with factions opposed to his rehabilitation in the court of public opinion, among them the Catholic Church. Fresh rumors were cooked up and circulated to perpetuate and legitimize further antagonism toward the officer's defenders.

"On more than one occasion, our fellow citizen has accused Freemasons of engineering Dreyfus' release. He continues to insist in casual conversation that his innocence has never been proven.

"What this citizen has no way of knowing -- or could be consciously disregarding -- is that Masonic lodges, not quite ready to open their doors to Jews at the time, had retreated behind their statutory shield during the 'Affair.' The founding principles of modern Freemasonry firmly oppose interference in matters of state. Sympathizing with Dreyfus, let alone negotiating on his behalf, would have violated Masonic protocols and envenomed the historic antipathy of the Church -- which was openly anti-Semitic and fiercely anti-Dreyfus -- toward the fraternity. Thus, Freemasons not only could not intervene, they responded with diffidence and irresolution in the face of gross injustice; and the Widow's Son was immolated, once again, at the altar of political expediency.

"The moral of this tale: History is written by historians. It is often falsified in the classroom, further distorted by subjective amateurs wed to ideology, not fact, and hopelessly vulgarized by filmmakers who take liberties on the assumption that fact somehow needs to be embellished by fantasy.

"The French Revolution was an extraordinarily complex affair, ignited by the antagonisms between the first two Estates, a bloated aristocracy and a corrupt and gluttonous clergy, and the third Estate, the crushing mass of dirt-poor, uneducated and downtrodden people whose antagonism was fueled by decades of abuse and frustration.

"Much like the Russian Revolution, which had already begun to simmer, the French Revolution was a genuine insurrection born from centuries of mis-management, corruption, oppression and exploitation of the people by small, all-powerful and brutal oligarchies.

"In 1789 France was a nation of twenty-six million. Society was made up of three distinct and grossly unequal groups. At the top was the aristocracy of the sword (some 500,000 people or about two percent of the population) families close to the throne, hangers-on and slackers. Next was the petty nobility, composed of provincial gentlemen of lesser means but matching affectation and greed, and the *nouveaux-riches* nobility, the *parvenus*, those who bought nobility titles but who, despite their wealth, were scorned by the bluebloods for their plebeian origins.

"The second tier was the clergy –- 120,000 strong, among them one hundred and thirty-nine bishops, also divided between high clergy (members of the aristocracy) and the common clergy -- both corrupt, depraved and decadent.

"Last was the Third Estate, the masses -- ninety-eight percent -- representing day laborers, farmers, peasants, craftsmen and a *petite bourgeoisie* composed of bankers, lawyers and trades people.

"The king's power was absolute, limitless and issued from no less an authority than God. The king hired and fired his cabinet at will. All power was centralized in Paris and in the hands of Louis XVI, a gutless kinglet who would have much preferred to fly kites or repair locks than govern. Injustice, ineptitude and fraudulence were rampant. Louis's remedy? He tightened the reins of power and subjected France to the kind of despotism then in vogue in Russia, Austria and Prussia.

"This was the twilight of the 18th century, the era of Enlightenment, and France was tired and wary of the ancient and traditional order in which the king reigned supreme, a parasitic clergy prayed for victory, and the rabble toiled and paid crippling taxes until they dropped. But this king was a bungling military strategist, his officers were inept and his spiritual advisers, fat and crooked, made a mockery of religion.

"Louis' prime minister, Jacques Necker, attempted to restore France's finances, severely crippled by its participation in America's war of independence. He suggested cutting the entitlements that the nobility received tax free from the crown. Threatened by Necker's sound but draconian scheme, the king's freeloaders, secular and religious, conspired against the prime minister and he was sidelined. Other fiscal reforms failed to repair the immense and growing gash in the public treasury. The nobles were not only unwilling to part with their stipends, they wanted to retain their political clout and dominance in society. The petty nobility, the bourgeoisie and the people, resenting their deprivations, sought to improve their lot and promulgate their rights. Rocked by scandals -- sex and fraud -- the high clergy was in a pitiful state. Resentful, but no less debauched, the low clergy was now ready to rebel against their superiors.

"Meanwhile, philosophers, writers, scientists -- Voltaire, Diderot, Rousseau, Saint-Simon and Lavoisier -- saw in revolution a weapon against the despotism of absolute monarchy and the clergy's fanaticism and cupidity.

"The ensuing uprising was less an act of insubordination against dictatorship than an insurrection against a grotesque class disparity between the haves and the have not. It was a social, not a political movement that purged France of hereditary kings and parasitical clergy. Given sufficient impetus, social movements eventually prevail.

"The economic crisis sweeping France accentuated the inequality between the classes. The rich got richer and the poor got poorer. Thousands died of hunger. It was obvious to most that France could not escape revolution. Would it be short or protracted, violent or peaceful? Would much needed reforms forestall the inevitable? Only the king, his queen, the blue-bloods, the knights and the princes of the Church could answer that, but they were all opposed to change.

"Louis hid behind his neurotic piety (and a bad case of phimosis). He neglected his wife in favor of hunting and tinkering with locks and clocks. He was drawn neither by royal duty, love, sex, politics, nor war, which he entrusted to pompous and ham-fisted generals. Inattentive to fact, deaf to reason, unwilling to heed advice, incapable of making decisions on his own, he took solace in his wife's opinion of him:

'Pauvre homme, il est bon -- poor man, he is kind.'

"Goodness in 1789 was apparently not enough. Marie-Antoinette, a spendthrift with a colossal disregard for the well being of her people, her reputation further sullied by the famous *Necklace Affair* and allegations of infidelity, became not only unpopular but loathed. The affair of the diamond necklace, you all have learned in school, was a mysterious and sordid incident involving Marie Antoinette, a cardinal, a con artist -- the famous charlatan Cagliostro, better known as Joseph Balsamo -- and a prostitute. The queen, whose reputation was already tarnished by gossip and scandal, was implicated in a crime that further increased the French people's disillusionment with the monarchy.

"A propos of the famous brioche quote, it's a myth. Marie-Antoinette was so out of touch with the lives of her subjects that she had no way of knowing whether they dined on moldy bread, escargots or filet mignon. Revisionists of all stripes have attempted to rehabilitate the queen -- or at least lend her a human visage. She was in fact a pretentious scatterbrain and a squanderer who, with her cuckold husband Louis' approval, ruined France. Some have argued that she was tried on trumped up charges. Indeed, Marie-Antoinette's trial had nothing to do with the legal definition of treason but everything to do with *treachery*, meaning deceitfulness, disloyalty and duplicity. Her accusers fittingly charged her (and Louis) with unscrupulousness; corruption; embezzlement; cruelty; a perverse disregard for the well being of the people; profligacy; avarice; squandering the national treasury; and when all was lost, flight to avoid prosecution.

"Modern France can well understand the hatred, the rage Louis and Marie-Antoinette's bankrupt, abject, merciless and dehumanizing reign provoked among the people. Some, among them the fellow citizen I keep mentioning but will not name, are still fixated on the royal heads that rolled into the wicker basket but they have no memory of the despair of the wretched masses or of the thousands of *Lettres de Cachet*, signed by the King and countersigned by princes of the Church, which sent innocent people, among them Huguenots, Jews, nonconformists and dissenters into exile or to the gallows.

"Much of the world has come to regard royalty as an anachronism, if not an obscenity. Perhaps evolution will endow the human brain with the capacity to regard organized religion as yet another form of entrapment by an elite engaged in its own preservation, as were the dynasties of thugs who called themselves kings. I know that the fellow citizen to whom I've been referring all along will recoil at the thought, but tradition is a poor excuse for the perpetuation of costly eccentricities. Time has come to recognize that what gives dignity to one individual ensures the dignity of all.

"In parting, Hieronymus Bosch, the artist behind the recent spasm of priestly rancor, said it all in his paintings five centuries ago. I urge my Fellow Freemasons and the public at large to discover what a mind free of absurd beliefs, an unerring eye, an attentive ear and a heart dedicated to knowledge and justice can do to make the world look at itself. Vive la France. Vive la République. Vive la Laïcité."

●

● ●

Grand Master Lelouch's nationally televised speech

triggers instant and feverish interest in Hieronymus Bosch. People flock to museums around Europe to gawk at his fantastical creations. Reproductions of his work sell in record numbers. The Louvre contacts the El Prado in Madrid, asking it to grant the temporary loan of several of his masterpieces. Books about the Flemish master fly off the shelves.

Lelouch's speech also stirs France's republican soul, eliciting editorials, essays and political cartoons eulogizing the innovative and civilizing changes brought on by the Revolution. Several newspapers, among them *Le Monde, Libération* and *L'Humanité*, publish retrospectives extolling secularism and urging untiring vigilance against the intrusion of the Church into affairs of state.

Archbishop Trente-Trois is apoplectic. He orders Le Calvaire "not to engage the enemy." He instructs priests throughout France to steer clear of the controversy and directs them to keep their sermons pastoral. He then convenes an emergency consistory. Father Hubert François de Ravaillac, Opus Dei's and the Knights of Malta's most promising star, will be all ears.

HIRAM FALLS

ON SUNDAY, AUGUST 9, 2009, prior to leading the recitation of the Angels with the faithful gathered in the courtyard of his summer residence at Castel Gandolfo, Pope Benedict XVI "meditates" on several saints who are commemorated during this period. One of them is Saint Teresa Benedicta of the Cross, better known as Edith Stein, who, *"consumed with love and won over by Christ,"* converted from Judaism, became a Carmelite nun and later perished at Auschwitz. From her, the Holy Father asserts,

> "We can learn the evangelical heroism that impels us to give our life fearlessly for the salvation of the soul. Love triumphs over death. All saints, but especially martyrs, are witnesses of God, who is Love: *Deus caritas est.*"

Glorifying conversion as a path to salvation, the pope's "meditation" does not allow for the possibility that Edith Stein died in a Nazi concentration camp because she was Jewish, not because she sacrificed herself, that her "martyrdom," like that of millions of her coreligionists, was that of a hated Jew, not because St. Teresa of Avila's story inspired her to take the veil. The most powerful man in the Church, the man who lives in Babylonian splendor, the commander-in-chief of an army of Swiss Guards, the holy mortal worshipped by more than one billion Catholics, then asks his audience to reflect on the *"profound divergences ... that have transformed human beings into gods."* He does not elaborate. Instead, he invites the faithful to come forward, kneel before him and kiss his blessed ring.

●

●　●

On that same day in August, Michel Montvert reflects in silence as he marks the death, four hundred and ninety-three years ago, of Hieronymus Bosch, one of his heroes, the artist who inventively and at the peril of his own life, exposed the *"profound divergences'* that continue to turn out false prophets and allow ambitious egomaniacs to exploit human stupidity.

Montvert raises his hands high above his head, lowers them in three distinct rhythmic motions and whispers, *"Is there no mercy for the Widow's Son?"* He remembers the distant expression, a mixture of sarcasm and controlled exasperation, in Bosch's surreptitious self-portraits.

●

●　●

A fortnight later, still on vacation at his summer palace, the pope asks the faithful to reflect on the Bread of Life Discourse in the Gospel of St. John, in which Jesus presents himself as

> "the bread of life ... which came down from heaven ... if anyone eats of this bread, he will live for ever: and the bread which I shall give for the life of the world is my flesh."

It is not without a hint of bitterness that Benedict XVI accuses "the Jews," who find the concept repulsive, of misinterpreting the message and distancing themselves from the messenger. Shifting from metaphor to vampirism, the pope then scolds "the world" for debating -- rather than swallowing whole -- Jesus' demented warning, *"...unless you eat the flesh of the Son of Man and drink his blood, you have no life in you."* He argues that Jesus, not given to compromise, has no cause to make himself understood, and he urges mankind to trust in the *"power of the Holy Spirit."* Rapt, seduced by this preposterous injunction, the faithful cross themselves at the very thought of feasting, even symbolically on the Son of Man.

Homo hominis lupus. Man is a wolf to man. He feeds on sheep.

●

● ●

On September 19, the first day of Rosh Hashanah, Jacques Lelouch, the Grand Master of the Grand Orient of France is pushed under the wheels of an oncoming train at the Saint-Paul Metro Station. His assailant melts into the crowd of rush-hour commuters and vanishes.

•

• •

The legend of *"Hiram, the Widow's Son,"* is the keystone of Freemasonry's ritualistic drama of the Third, or Master's Degree. When Solomon, King of Israel, undertook the building of the Temple in Jerusalem, he asked King Hiram of Tyre for materials and architectural expertise. King Hiram, in exchange for corn, oil and wine, sent Solomon cedar trees from the forests of Lebanon and appointed a skilled worker, or artificer, to oversee the project. This story appears in the Old Testament (Kings, 1-7) and (Chronicles, 11-2). An artisan, also named Hiram, is referred to as *"the son of a widow of the tribe of Naftali"* whose husband hailed from Tyre. This feature of the Masonic legend comes from Scriptures. But the story staged by Freemasons has a tragically different twist and is inspired to impart symbolic and life-altering lessons. Hiram Abiff (Hebrew for "father") worked for Solomon in Jerusalem as the Master of the Works, or chief architect and builder. More than 85,000 people were employed in the erection of the Temple, which took seven years to complete.

Workmen who labored faithfully were promised to be elevated to the status of Master Mason. Some time before the Temple's completion, several workmen became impatient and demanded the promotion they had been promised. They also sought to obtain the higher wages and fringe benefits accorded to Master Masons and conspired to extort them from Hiram Abiff. Resisting their threats, Hiram rejected their demands. Reminding them of their obligations to King Solomon, he insisted that they honor the contracts by which he and they were bound. Three of them, more cunning and brutal than the others plotted to attack Master Hiram and force the concessions he denied them. Hiram stood firm and the three murdered him in the unfinished Temple.

The legend of Hiram is one of the most impressive ritualistic dramas of all time. Tenuous evidence, some deduced from ancient art, some found in arcane medieval texts, suggests that the story of Hiram may have been known to operative Masons as early as the Middle Ages. Perhaps the legend is a reworking of some medieval mystery play whose original may have been secreted in some private library or forgotten amid the debris of an ancient building.

Regardless of its origins, the drama of Hiram is a representation of the eternal conflict between men, of individuals pitted against the evil forces embodied in other men. The enemies Hiram faces are symbols of the lusts and passions and failures of the human spirit. Seen in that light, Hiram's violent death is also his triumph -- the resurrection of truth over ignorance. The enriching significance of the legend of Hiram is that it continues to stir men to serve the Truth by steadfastly keeping its flame burning bright and in full view of those who would shield their eyes from it.

Seen in the light of contemporary history, the assassination of Manuel Albeniz and Jacques Lelouch, as was that of Hiram Abiff, can also be construed as a grotesque act of censorship. The assassins were less interested in obtaining the "secrets" of a Master Mason as they were in preventing the dissemination and popularization of the freethinking ideals they impart.

EPILOGUE

A LONE LETTER to the editor in *Le Monde* sums up Lelouch's murder with the pithiest of epitaphs: *"Humans are just not nice."* Montvert, who has lost two friends and Brother Freemasons, first Albeniz, then Lelouch, agrees. But what does this self-evident truth say about the crime, about the criminal, about his motives, about the sadism of man? What does it express other than some letter writer's fondness for clichés?

The writer is right, of course, but his summation is as shallow as it is fragmentary. Yes, we are not "nice" but we are unique. We possess seeds of genius and inspiration. Hidden deep in our subconscious teem the viruses of jealousy, greed, spite and aggression. Astonishing acts of creativity are accompanied by surges of unspeakable evil.

We pulverized Nagasaki and Hiroshima and have since left our footsteps on the Moon. We used napalm and Agent Orange in Vietnam, experimented with LSD and syphilis on unwary citizens and landed robotic explorers on Mars. We fought to "liberate" some nations from the yoke of oppression while ignoring slavery in other parts of the world. We fed the hungry in areas of strategic importance and let others starve to death. We carried the Cross in one hand and brandished the sword in the other. We sired Euripides and Shakespeare, Bach and Beethoven, Michelangelo and Van Gogh, Galileo and Einstein ... and spawned Attila and Hitler, Stalin and Mao, Pol Pot and Saddam, Torquemada and Hubert de Ravaillaic.

Montvert finds no contradiction in these incongruities, however jarring the contrast between them. He accepts with equal dispassion both the wretchedness and the sublime transcendence of the human spirit. Leaning against the forged iron railing of his balcony, surrounded by window-boxes brimming with geraniums, he gazes at his beloved Paris. Then scenes from his childhood blur the heavenly landscape.

June 14, 1940. The Germans had crossed the ancient city gates. Huge flags -- a black swastika on a field of crimson and white -- were hoisted over palaces and public buildings, replacing the French tricolor. German soldiers were seen buffing their boots with it, arousing laughter among the troops.

Paris had been overpowered. A ghastly silence hovered over the once bustling narrow cobbled streets of the old part of town. It was as if the city had lost its soul. Elsewhere, on Place Pigalle, on the Champs Elysées, in the open vastness of the Place de la Concorde, small groups of Parisians, including priests, greeted and feted the invaders. Many volunteered their services. Others offered their bodies for bread or wine or money to expiate France's fervid capitulation in a symbolic act of self-immolation.

He remembered seeing vast numbers of Parisians standing motionless, weeping openly, a quiet rage burning in their eyes as German soldiers -- the reincarnated Sons of Darkness -- strutted freely in the magnificent but now dimmed City of Light. He would never forget their tears. And he remembered taking his father's hand and huddling next to him for warmth and reassurance. Sensing disquiet, his father had picked him up and held him in his arms. He had smiled and pressed him closer to his heart, and Montvert saw sadness in his father's face, sadness and fear.

Montvert was three.

He was now an old man. Time had done little to quiet the inner echoes of primal cynicism that had escorted him since childhood. He had sailed the seven seas, flown on the Concorde, scaled Mayan tabernacles, probed the Kabbalah's dizzying and mazelike realm, marveled at the erotic carvings of the Khajuraho temples in India, dived in the amethyst waters of the gulf of Aqaba, combed the ruins of the ancient community in Qumran, studied the ancient scrolls.

●

● ●

As Montvert stood on the ruins of the millennia-old monastery, shimmering in the afterglow of dawn, suspended between the amethyst sky and the brackish waters of the Dead Sea, the furrowed mountains of Moab and Gilead had loomed in the distance, bleak, barren. Rolling in from the Mediterranean, passing over Bethlehem and Hebron, a rare cluster of rain-swollen clouds had surrendered its precious life-bearing gift. It was only a sprinkle but together with the morning dew the welcome shower, Montvert knew, would energize the date palms and the neatly tended patches of barley and wheat. Here in the Great Rift, 390 meters below sea level -- the lowest point on Earth -- grainfield was not the golden ocean of swaying corn that dwarfed the harvester in the Valley of Jezreel or the coastal plains of Sharon. Here the men had to stoop and pluck the plant by its roots. The sheaves were squat, short-stalked and sparsely leafed but the ears were full. There would be bread for all.

Amplified by the great stillness hovering over mangled bluffs and escarpments, riding on the wings of an occasional rush of hot, dry wind, the surefooted hoof beat of a clan of ibexes resonated in the distance. Wary, their scimitar-shaped horns poised like antennae, their quivering nostrils probing the scorching updrafts, Montvert had seen them come to drink from weather-worn shallow limestone basins. Catching a whiff of danger in the air, they had vaulted from boulder to boulder, leaving a pungent trail of musk behind them.

Down below, dressed in white linen robes, lost in their apocalyptic incantations, men had descended single-file into a pool fed by runoff rainwater. A narrow, ankle-high berm in the center of a steep stairwell had separated the cleansed from those still awaiting purification. Such ritual ablutions, it was written, were repeated when the Sun reached its meridian height, and just before it sank behind the craggy ramparts and cast long cooling shadows upon the old settlement.

A simple meal had been shared, freshly laundered

communal vestments distributed. Standing on the top landing of the two-story watchtower commanding the Dead Sea's darkening, glassy surface, a lonely figure bent by age had peered at the horizon through slits worked into meter-thick cut stone. Like the ibexes now resting in their lairs, the old man had grown uneasy. The world is evil, the old rabbi had whispered to himself. Greed and lust mock the God of all creation. That such a world should be sundered is obvious. That the end was near seemed nowhere more manifest than in this dreadful chasm, halfway between the Bitter Lake and the wretched cliffs disfigured by the sun's scorching breath. Was it not in this accursed region, patriarchal texts recount -- in Sodom and in Gomorra -- that man laid the scene of God's fury? What will it be this time? Lightning? Torrential rain? Floods? Another deadly tremor? Earthquakes had badly damaged the life-bearing aqueducts, their course forever diverted.

Tugging at the old rabbi's soul as no prophecy had done before was the fear that other forces were now at play. No, the threat came not from the slumbering peaks of Moab where his anxious gaze had rested. It would descend instead, like a stream of crazed scorpions and asps fleeing a fire, from Jerusalem, a day's journey to the northwest. So far, the Roman occupation of Judea had been uneventful. Roman rulers were as fair as they were rapacious and scarcely greedier than the native Jewish kings. Yet, tension between Jews and Romans was high. With hundreds of fabulous deities orchestrating their lives, the Romans had regarded monotheism as an aberration. For their part, the Jews could not tolerate the blasphemy of idolatry. Jew was disdainful of Roman, Roman was contemptuous of Jew. Pontius Pilate was outraged by the Jews' defiance of Roman might. Charges of paganism bewildered him. Caligula, his sanguinary successor, ordered that his effigy be erected in Solomon's Temple, in Jerusalem. His assassination prevented the desecration from taking place.

As calamity followed calamity, the men in Qumran were now certain that the End of Days, was at hand, that the Anointed One, the spiritual savior prophesied by Isaiah and longed for by the Jews, the Messiah of lore and prayer, was drawing near. The moon had not yet *"turned to blood,"* nor had the stars tumbled from their heavenly perch, but destruction was upon the *"evil ones"* who had cowed Israel, and it was time for Yahweh to lead the Sons of Light in their final assault against the Sons of Darkness.

In preparation for this fateful contest, animated by its urgency, the scribes had worked from dawn to dusk, from sunset to the cock's earliest crow in the windowless scriptorium. There, they had recopied old manuscripts, mended sacred scrolls and sealed them in earthen jars that the younger men would hide in the caves dotting the surrounding cliffs. One day, the covenanters would return and retrieve their beloved Torah, manuals and commentaries. By then, the old sage mused, the Teacher of Righteousness would have defeated Belial, and the emissary of Aaron and Israel would preside over the sacred meal, and divine ordinance would rule the land. But first he and his brothers would have to disperse. The exodus, yet another in a succession of hasty retreats and lengthy exiles, would take some south to Masada and the wilderness beyond, perhaps as far as Goshen where the patriarchs once dwelt. Others would cross the Jordan and join caravans up to the fertile valleys of the Tigris and Euphrates. Others yet, roused by a newfangled apostolic fervor, would trek back to western Judea and Samaria, to spread the word and gain new converts.

The year was 3828 (68 C.E.) and, unbeknownst to these ascetic Jews, descendants of over fifteen generations of a pious, fiercely independent Hasidic sect known as the Essenes, this would be the last time they would ever see Qumran. It would take nearly two thousand years -- and a fortuitous act of curiosity by a young Bedouin in 1947 -- to exhume the Essenes from the cinders of history. Ironically but to no one's surprise, their resurrection would cause great consternation in some circles and set off a cascade of stormy debates fed by ego and religious fundamentalism at the expense of scholarship.

•

•   •

Sixty-two years after the discovery of the Dead Sea Scrolls, Montvert, the globe-trotting scholar and incorrigible iconoclast, had triggered a similar tidal wave of controversy and unease. But this time the uproar had less to do with academic disputes than with the politics of conflicting ideologies. In resurrecting Hieronymus Bosch, he had opened a Pandora's Box of acrimony, resentment and vengeance that further radicalized a phalanx of vindictive zealots and claimed two lives.

The inane letter to the editor had irked Montvert, prompting him, as was his custom when irked, to strike back. Published in *Le Monde*, measured and controlled, his all-purpose riposte mentioned neither Bosch nor Albeniz or Lelouch but it contained verities that were as irrefutable as they were apt to reignite the odium he and his late friends and Brothers had inspired.

There was a pattern to these spontaneous rejoinders. Gadfly-extraordinaire, bewitched by art, cursed with an urge to write, no, *to indict*, lured by controversy, Montvert had reinvented himself over the years: part activist, part rabble-rouser. He was less interested in explicating than in exposing, debunking, in finding the tiniest of stains in the purest driven snow. The pleasure he derived from such commerce far exceeded any possible urge to inform. He treated fact as a prop. It was the mood, the emotions, the color his words conveyed, the consternation or the outrage they were apt to engender, that made him reach for a pen, not reverence for the fourth estate, nor a fondness for the reader. When not engaged in scholarly discourse, he was busy causing unease and discomfiture -- reminding the forgetful and the smug that the emperor has no clothes, keeping the son of a bitch stripped long enough for all to see him bare-assed and trembling, stinging and confounding men blinded by their own self-induced myopia.

Montvert had paid dearly for indulging his vice -- it cost him promotions and friendships, it isolated him and earned him threats -- but he would remain habituated, less for the fleeting high it produced than out of regard for all the unpopular causes he had espoused, some out of conviction, others out of spite.

Another piece he drafted for publication, this time in *L'Humanité*, posited that if lies imprison the mind, then the truth sets it free, adding that what people who disagree with this truism loudly proclaim is that "certain inconvenient truths," like sleeping dogs, are best left undisturbed. He had further proposed that any attempt to entomb the truth, however wrenching, embarrassing or dangerous it might be, is the essence of evil; that silence in the face of misdeeds invites more self-censorship and more misdeeds. He had then itemized what he openly professed to be his core beliefs:

- Morality predates religion.
- The subconscious is susceptible to manipulation.
- Nationalism, chauvinism and religiosity are attitudes forcibly nailed into unpolluted psyches then hammered through repetition and the discipline of fear.
- Killers are made, not sired.
- Faith and reason are mutually exclusive.
- Ignorance and intellectual sloth keep alive the conflict between secular humanism and religion, between sanity and psychosis.
- Those who seek the truth are infinitely closer to it than those who claim to have found it.
- None is as ignorant as he who chooses not to know. Willful myopia subverts good judgment and defiles the truth.
- Everybody has opinions. Much of our mental

constructs are erected on a vast scaffolding of dogmas -- generally someone else's. We adopt these beliefs and attitudes, we cling to them because they encourage us not to think, because they shield us from what we fear most -- the cold, naked truth -- because they keep us warm and cozy in our self-created doctrinal cocoons.

- There are more opinions than facts and we are enamored of them. Opinions blithely disregard, defy and, if need be, corrupt the truth. Tainted fruits of ignorance and self-delusion, opinions often overlook faulty data or perpetuate arguments riddled with ideological monstrosities. Opinions, like inflexible beliefs, shield us from the risks of personal experience. Every time we inhale a wisp of fact, we exhale a gust of inferences.

- In the mouths of demagogues, personal convictions assume dangerous dimensions: They are not what can be borne out by observation or logical deduction but what suits ingrained doctrines. Regurgitated by imbeciles, they are promptly espoused by other imbeciles.

- Only those willing to question the validity of "conventional wisdom" can ever get closer to the truth. Fallacious reasoning, licit as it might be, is a greater enemy of truth than an outright lie. It is the prison in which we lock ourselves to feign a clear conscience. As someone once remarked, a clear conscience is usually the sign of a very bad memory.

- Troublesome facts, computed by rational minds,

are more useful than myths peddled by uninformed crusaders. When flock mentality is at play,
it is the myths, alas, that capture the imagination
of the majority. Inflexible convictions render men
blind, arrogant and, carried to the extreme, mad.

And, in an oblique reference to Hieronymus Bosch, he
had put forward that --

- True art is experimental. When it ceases to
  reinvent itself, to enchant, amuse or scandalize, or
  when it veers from the truth, it is no longer art.

In a rare moment of self-restraint, Montvert shelved the
piece. It needed more work. He would never get a chance
to submit it.

●
● ●

Montvert turned instead to a quatrain he had penned a
fortnight earlier -- he called it his "overture" to a short
essay on the role of art in the portrayal and interpretation
of psychosis:

> What have his weary eyes seen?
> Why this pallor upon his face?
> He dipped his brush in the bowels of Hell
> and unmasked the human race.

What Hieronymus Bosch's weary eyes beheld is

preamble and afterthought, prelude and climax in an age of nascent reason and persistent folly. Tried and convicted for heresy, Jacques de Mollay, Grand Master of the Knights Templar, and Joan of Arc had long since been burned at the stake. More witch-hunts would follow. Barely concluded, the One Hundred-Year War would keep alive the political and religious conflict between England and France. It would take nearly four hundred years for the enmity to cease. The plague, cholera, dysentery and a host of venereal diseases would claim untold thousands in their wake.

Religious friction, many elements of which resulted from an attempt by some to oxygenate the Church and by others to further fossilize it, threatened to destroy the very fabric of Christianity. The armies of King Francis the First, in a campaign billed as a *"crusade to the glory of Christ,"* exterminated nearly all the members of a Calvinist sect in northern Italy. Light prevailed for a time and its radiance guided the uncommon man. But the light vacillated anew, fanned by doctrinal discord and greed and cultural narcissism. Dedicated to validating Copernicus' heliocentric theory, Galileo would be charged with blasphemy and forced to recant. The St. Bartholomew's Day Massacre would destroy an entire generation of Huguenot leadership. Fearing for his throne (and his head), French King Henri IV, a Protestant, would cravenly abjures his faith and convert to Catholicism.

In that 60-year period that bridges the Middle Ages and early Renaissance was born, lived and died a remarkable man, an astute observer of human folly, an incomparable artist, the undisputed father of Surrealism and, as the subtle clues that season his eerie renditions suggest, a visionary of uncommon perspicacity.

What Bosch recorded and foretold in his haunting work is the recurring death of reason. In the thousand faces of human bestiality his brush enlivens can be glimpsed the ferocity and injustices of future nightmares: Colonialism. Slavery. Famine. Pestilence. Wars of "liberation." Wars of subjugation. Wars of territorial expansion. Fratricide. "Holy" wars. Wars to end all wars. Genocide. Weapons of mass destruction. Death squads. Intolerance. Segregation. Sectarian strife. Foreign domination. The rise and radicalization of theocracy. Terrorism in the service of God. The Torah and occupation and expulsion and dispossession. The cross and the sword. The Koran and the scimitar.

•

• •

On September 27, 2009, Pope Benedict XVI urges a crowd of 120,000 worshippers at an open-air Mass in the Czech Republic, one of Europe's most secular nations, to remain faithful to religious tradition.

> "History has demonstrated the absurdities to which man descends when he excludes God for the horizon of his choices and actions."

The pope does not bother to enumerate the absurdities and the horrors to which man descends in the service of

God.

The day before, as he addressed politicians and diplomats in Prague, a large arachnid cruised on the pope's white robes. When it reached his ear, Benedict gave it a swat but it didn't go away; it reappeared on his left shoulder and scampered down his robe. As the pontiff left the medieval Prague Castle's ornate Spanish Hall, the spider could be seen hanging from a stand of web.

Spiders, like men, are often feared and scorned. Unlike popes, they do serve a purpose. Spiders are not parasites. They work hard for their dinner.

●

● ●

On October 1st, Montvert receives an undated, unsigned letter. Scribbled to simulate a child's scrawl, it quotes from one of the New Testament's most anti-Judaic rants:

> Ye are of your father the devil and the lusts of your father ye will do. He was a murderer from the beginning, and abode not in the truth, because there is no truth in him. When he speaketh a lie, he speaketh of his own for he is a liar, and the father of it. (John, 8:44).

The missive then plucks a paragraph from Romans (2:5):

> But because of your stubbornness and your unrepentant heart, you are storing up wrath for

yourselves in the day of wrath, when God's righteous judgment is revealed.

It ends on an ominous note:

And the Lord smote Albeniz and Lelouch. In the name of Almighty God, thou shalt be next.

Montvert smiles. Barbarism and absurdity are not mutually exclusive. He also reminds himself that whistle-blowers are not spurned, persecuted or marked for death because they enjoy the blood sport of exhuming the truth but because they fling it, like excrement, in the eyes of those who fear it most.

•
• •

Two days later, in celebration of Armed Forces Day, the Virgin of Suyapa, Honduras's most sacred religious icon, is paraded in the streets of Tegucigalpa. This obnoxious spectacle, following the military coup that ousted, at gunpoint and in his pajamas, the constitutionally elected president of Honduras, Manuel Zelaya, epitomizes the servility of the Church vis-à-vis a de facto, illegal and crooked minority regime that usurped power with the help of one of the most oppressive and ruthless military establishments in Central America.

On that same day, as dusk wraps Paris in a chilly embrace, Montvert is assassinated. Laying in wait on Place Du Tertre, where Montvert often dined, Hubert de

Ravaillac, dressed in civilian attire, lunges at Lelouch as he is about to enter the *Au Clairon des Chasseurs* restaurant and stabs him repeatedly in the heart with a large Masonic ceremonial compass. He flees on foot but is quickly apprehended. Narrowly escaping lynching by horrified passersby, he is whisked away by police and taken to the nearest *commissariat*.

Agitated and haughty, licking his blood-stained hands, de Ravaillac tells interrogators that the Virgin Mary had instructed him to kill Lelouch, a heretic, a Jew and a Freemason.

As Montvert lay dying in a widening pool of his own blood, a priest who happened to be passing by administers the last rites, unaware that Montvert is a Jew and an atheist. With life slowly ebbing, like an apparition emerging from the fog, a singular moment lived in the antiquity of his childhood materializes before his eyes.

Attacks on German soldiers during the occupation of France were swiftly countered with public executions. Staged to set an example and deter further aggression against the occupier, these grisly pageants also palliated the enemy's frustration while satisfying its thirst for vengeance. One morning, ten men, eight of them veterans of the First World War, were dragged to the village square, lined up against the church wall and shot to avenge the murder of a German officer who had been screwing the baker's daughter. Montvert saw them crumple, lifeless, on the cobbled sidewalk. Their mission accomplished, ten pink-faced young men placed their rifles on their shoulders, spun on their heels and marched away, single file, expressionless, robot-like in their mustard-brown uniforms. Montvert had stared at the pitiful mass of inert, crumpled bodies, blood oozing from their open mouths, their eyes staring in the void, like the eyes of a doll. He also remembered saying to himself over and over that he'd been treated to a grotesque but otherwise meaningless spectacle, a dramatization of unimaginable realism, something akin to cinema. It began to rain and a steady downpour washed away the blood as onlookers scattered and dissolved in a gray sulfur-laden mist. Framed in the doorway of the old stone Gothic church, a priest crossed himself three times then sanctified the scene of the carnage with a few drops of "holy" water.

Montvert was five.

A lifetime later, a black-robed man kneels by Montvert's side and offers him the *viaticum*, "provisions for the journey beyond." A vague grin parts Montvert's lips.

"*Satis,*" he murmurs in Latin before expiring. "Enough."

•

• •

Bishop Touvier intercedes and on advice of court-appointed psychiatrists, Hubert de Ravaillac is transferred to Esquirol Hospital, outside Paris, site of the famous 350-year-old insane asylum also known as Charenton.

Montvert's violent death, as had that of Grand Master Lelouch, receives discreet coverage. The media, to prevent possible violence against innocent clerics, refrain from identifying his assassin. Terse news reports characterize the incident as "a senseless homicide" and describe the perpetrator as a "drifter, a raving and incurable lunatic destined to die in confinement."

In time, the clamor subsides and the matter is forgotten. France, its passions briefly stirred, regains its urbane and bon-vivant bearing. Esteemed in life, mourned in death, Jacques Lelouch, Manuel Albeniz and Michel Montvert fade from memory, their names and legacy displaced and eclipsed by the fad or the bugaboo of the hour.

Masonic lodges continue to initiate neophytes who will labor on behalf of peace and social justice. The Church, its delicate ego bruised, lays low. Seminarians enter the priesthood in diminishing numbers. Some retreat to monasteries where they while away the hours praying for unattainable ideals. Some leave the orders, get married and have children who will serve the state and die on distant battlefields. Some, throbbing with religious fervor, will wage holy wars of their own. Freethinkers will defy them and expose their hideous schemes.

And, after enjoying an ephemeral burst of renewed attention, Hieronymus Bosch, the futurist, the prodigious "inventor," the artist who warned against greed, lust and folly, Bosch, born in an ancient fortified city whose entire Jewish population was burned alive in the 13th century and where the wars of the Reformation would soon change the course of history, Bosch, who never lived to see his hometown transformed into a Nazi internment camp -- but could have foreseen it -- Bosch, the Alchemical Man who mocked the Church in a way only the Church could understand, was quietly returned to the relative obscurity from which he had all too briefly been plucked.

•

•   •

When it comes to stylish interments, no one outshines the Vatican, which buried all hopes of reunification or even meaningful dialogue with the Church of England when it announced, on October 20, 2009, that it would now welcome whole groups of Anglicans, their bishops, liturgies and even -- oh, hell, if they must absolutely have them -- their wives, to the Roman Catholic Church. This is a huge coup for Rome. It manages to publicly humiliate Rowan Williams, Archbishop of Canterbury, the symbolic head of the Anglican Church, to vilify its adherents and to exploit the ideological divisions that cleave Christendom. As the British daily, The Guardian, so astutely points out,

"God always did move in mysterious ways."

•

•   •

On November 3rd, Saint Malachy Day, Hubert de Ravaillac slips off his horsehair nightshirt. Naked, trembling with anticipation, he falls to his knees. Turning his gaze toward a point in space where God, Jesus and all the saints in heaven are said to dwell, he lunges forward and impales himself on the point of a crucifix he had sharpened for the occasion on the bare stone floor of his cell. Excruciating pain turns grimace to ecstatic smile as his entrails spill to the ground. He wraps his bloodied arms around his shoulders in a final farewell embrace then crumples lifeless in a pool of gore and squirming viscera.

Self-hatred is the grandest of love affairs.

No one knows for sure whether the 26-year-old priest was lucid enough to realize that he had spent the last three months of his life in the very same gloomy, damp chamber where, in 1814, after thirteen years of internment, the ill-famed but brilliant satirist and social commentator, Donatien Alphonse-François Marquis de Sade, who wrote, *"God is a monster; religion is the cradle of despotism,"* expired at the age of 74. It was the despotism of religion, the decadence of the aristocracy and the sleaze of the clergy that aristocrat de Sade railed against in his salacious novels and serious essays, none of which the young priest would have read -- or admitted to having read.

De Ravaillac's Shakespearean suicide is ignored. The press is busy covering a world ravaged by political corruption, crippling economic downturns, urban violence, ethnic strife, disease, famine and war. At his parents' request, his remains are cremated and his ashes are entombed in the family crypt.

The pope mourns his passing and prays for his soul.

Also on November 3rd, Israeli authorities announce the arrest of American-born Yaakov "Jack" Teitel, 37, a West Bank settler and religious fanatic with a 12-year history of terrorist attacks and murder plots against Arabs, including an east Jerusalem cab driver and a Palestinian shepherd. Teitel, who also targeted homosexuals, leftists and pacifists, sees himself as an emissary of God sent to Earth to eradicate all the profanities heaped upon the Almighty.

Some say he's crazy. Others, perched on the stolen Palestinian headlands that ring the "City of Peace," hail him as a martyr and call on the Almighty to heap all manner of calamities upon his censors.

So much for fellowship and ecumenism and the brotherhood of man.

POSTSCRIPT

THE UNTHINKABLE IS often preceded by the deceptive stillness of complacency. So, on November 5, a lone gunman opened fire in the Soldier Readiness Center at Fort Hood, Texas, killing thirteen people and injuring ten others. The gunman, U.S.-born Major Nidal Malik Hasan, a U.S. Army psychiatrist of Palestinian descent, had appeared on the radar of federal authorities at least six months before the deadly assault. Internet postings by Hasan spoke of his frustration with the military establishment and his opposition to U.S. involvement in Iraq and Afghanistan. Private conversations hinted at his deepening devotion to Islam. Seriously wounded in the incident by civilian police officers, now paralyzed from the waist down, he has since been charged with murder.

Hasan likened suicide bombers to soldiers who throw themselves on a grenade to save their comrades and sacrifice their lives for a "more noble cause." He declared that Muslims must stand up and fight against the "aggressor." The aggressor, it turned out, is the U.S., not the insurgency that rose in response to U.S. military action. Then he boasted, *I'm a Muslim first and an American second.*" Abstraction turned to paranoia when he asked *"whether the war on terror is a war against Islam."*

None of these tell-tale warning signs elicited more than passing curiosity. Nor did they prompt an investigation. No one had the imagination or instinct to decipher the clues Hasan left behind. He was in the throes of a gripping spiritual dilemma but no one found the courage to acknowledge that religion can transform men into crucibles of hatred, societies into citadels of bigotry.

The suspect's brother, Eyad Hasan, released a statement which expressed his family's "shock and disbelief":

"I've known my brother Nidal to be a peaceful, loving and compassionate person who never committed an act of violence and was always known to be a good, law-abiding citizen."

Platitude or irreconcilable truth? We may never know.

What remains unsaid at this writing is that Major Hasan's dastardly act was the predictable consequence of religion carried to its aberrant extreme; that history is peppered with gruesome instances of bestiality perpetrated for the glory of God. Somehow, no one dares qualify the Fort Hood incident, this latest manifestation of insanity, as the offspring of religious intolerance and fanaticism. *God forbid,* (pardon the expression), we should hurt the feelings of popes and rabbis and imams and their flock by suggesting that religion, in the best of cases, is an opiate that numbs all reason and, at worst, a sickness of the mind and a scourge. No one in the press or in intimate conversations will concede that no religion truly advocates peace and love -- except toward its own co-religionists. No one has the scruples to remember that Christianity was the first to wage wars of religion against Jews and Muslims.

I have read the Koran forward and backward and found nothing that advocates, even remotely, the kind of barbarism perpetrated by the jihadists. Alas, some of the language is so sublimely vague or figurative that it can easily be misinterpreted or distorted.

What is tragic about Major Hasan, a psychiatrist, is that he was unable to diagnose, let alone forestall, his own long simmering psychosis. Shamefully, despite glaring evidence of his conflicted loyalties, no one around him, not the military, not his fellow physicians, not his neighbors had the presence of mind to sound the alarm.

Engaged in inane conjectures, Americans are now wringing their hands yet again asking *"Why"* instead of pointing fingers at the real culprit: A love of God so intense and so all-consuming that it will inspire the cold-blooded murder of God's own "creation."

•

• •

On November 8, Pope Benedict XVI visits Brescia in northern Italy to pay tribute to his predecessor, the late Pope Paul VI. In a homily spiced with anti-Jewish allusions about Jesus' distaste for *"rabbinical disputations, improper practices in the Temple in Jerusalem"* and the hypocrisy of the ancient scribes who, *"while displaying great piety, are exploiting the poor and imposing obligations they themselves do not observe."* Look who's talking.

Unembellished by the sublime, the ridiculous shows its face on November 13 as a fanatical Muslim group launches a massive and boisterous demonstration in London demanding that *sharia* law be imposed in Britain. Calling for the dismantling of the British legal system, demonstrators hold placards proclaiming that *"communism is dead, capitalism is dying, Islam is the way for revival,"* and warning that *"Islam will dominate the world."* A poster-sized photo of Buckingham Palace shows what the royal residence will look like once it is transformed into a mosque.

Across the "pond," Michael Freund writes an inflammatory editorial in the right-wing, Brooklyn-based *The Jewish Press* calling for the faithful not to be intimidated by Muslim grievances and inciting them to worship at Temple Mount, one of Islam's most sacred shrines. Freund also encourages American Jews to buy homes in the Israeli-occupied territories, and urges Israelis to keep Jerusalem "Jewish."

In Washington, hard-right conservatives tell South Carolina Republican Congressman Bob Inglis that they are willing to let people who don't have health insurance *"die on the steps of hospitals"* to make a point about the problem of *"free riders."* Inglis, who is no flaming liberal, retorts:

"A guy named Jesus had some things to say about these kinds of concepts. I don't want to live in a society that lets a few test cases die on the steps of a hospital."

At about the same time, Mexican police arrest a 78-year-old man for killing a woman he swore was a witch who had cast a spell on him.

•

• •

Gathering beneath Michelangelo's Last Judgment in the Sistine Chapel on November 21, the Holy Father addresses a group of 250 artists from across the world -- painters, sculptors, architects, writers, poets, musicians, actors and directors. The aim of the meeting is to *"express the Church's friendship with the world of art"* and to encourage new opportunities for *"collaboration."*

No one would blame *"the various distinguished personalities present"* for questioning the Pope's sincerity, not to mention the Church's motives for such dramatic spectacle of self-promotion. After all, director Ron Howard fell out of favor with the Vatican and scores of movies, among them The Tin Drum. Lolita, The Last Temptation of Christ, The Da Vinci Code and its sequel, Angels and Demons are still banned. Hundreds of prestigious authors, including Rabelais, Voltaire, Descartes, Gide, de Beauvoir, Defoe, Swift, Graham Greene and Sartre figure prominently in the Vatican's Index, as are such literary gems as Hugo's Notre Dame de Paris, Flaubert's Madame Bovary and Boccaccio's Decameron.

•

•   •

A report released on November 26, 2009 by the Dublin Archdiocese Commission of Investigations acknowledges that [habitual]

> "clerical child sexual abuse was covered up by the Archdiocese of Dublin and other Church authorities."

The 720-page document asserts that the Diocese was

> "preoccupied ... with the maintenance of secrecy, the avoidance of scandal, the protection of the reputation of the Church, and the preservation of its assets.... It is abundantly clear that sexual abuse by clerics was widespread.
> "One priest admitted to sexually molesting more than 100 children; another confessed that he had abused children 'fortnightly' for over 25 years."

The report shoots down the notion that church leadership was unaware of the problem:

> "The taking out of insurance was an act proving knowledge of child sexual abuse as a potential danger to the Archdiocese."

•

•   •

On Sunday, 29 November, the First Sunday of Advent and of the new Liturgical Year, prior to leading the recitation of the Angelus, Pope Benedict XVI comments on "this Season, a period of preparation for the Lord's birth." Quoting from Luke (21:28) he affirms:

> "Whoever yearns for freedom, justice, and peace may rise again and raise his head, for in Christ liberation is drawing near."

Somehow, that 2,000-year-old promise has failed to deliver tangible results. The "Savior" has saved nothing. Convulsing under rising waves of hatred, ignorance, stupidity and superstition, racked by mounting violence, the world still awaits liberation. Russia is drowning in alcoholism. AIDS ravages Africa. In defiance of half-hearted reprimands, Sudan pursues its genocidal objectives. Poverty, despair, ethnic strife and shifting allegiances inspire massacres in the Philippines. In Israeli occupied territories, Palestinians are fighting to preserve increasingly shrinking fragments of their homeland. Global warming puts the arctic on thin ice and threatens to engulf coastal areas and dozens of islands around the globe. The U.S. clings to the unchallenged two-party-system -- both parties the flip sides of the same tarnished coin, both indistinguishable one from the other except for the partisanships and antipathies they inspire in their respective camps, both tied to corporate wealth, both intent of blocking meaningful reform in the name of capitalism, both involved in larceny against the poor. The gap between the haves and the have not continues to widen.

•

•   •

As the year 2009 draws to a close, citing well-worn myths, among them that Freemasons worship Lucifer, several Protestant denominations known for their abhorrence of secular values, warn their congregants not join Masonic lodges. They include the all-powerful Southern Baptist Convention, The Society of Friends, the Seventh-day Adventist Church, the Salvation Army, the Mennonites and the Evangelical Lutheran Synod.

Sic transit Gloria mundi.

ACKNOWLEDGMENTS

THIS BOOK WAS CONCEIVED long before I set out to construct it piece by piece from a patchwork of recurring childhood reminiscences, random musings hastily recorded in the dead of night and simmering emotions spiced up by the steady pace of history endlessly repeated. Several life-altering events and a harvest of images and insights gleaned during my years as an itinerant journalist also contributed to its protracted and painful gestation.

I must confess that when I decided to give this project wings, I was seduced by the notion that I would be penning the book I always wanted to read, an irreverent, vexing polemic -- part exposé, part history, part satire, part plausible conjecture -- a tract that could somehow help galvanize a world mired in myth and sanctified deception. Fighting windmills, as the Man of La Mancha noted after two, possibly three valiant quests, is pointless. The "giants" of blind faith, conformity and entrenched tradition are formidable foes, and common sense is swiftly submerged in the quicksand of fanaticism and ideological rigidity.

As I reviewed the manuscript one last time in search of stray typos and skewed syntax, I was seized with the notion that intellectual inertia can bring any forward momentum to a dead stop. From there, it was a short step to recalling the cynical French expression my old friend, mentor and alter ego Montvert was fond of quoting, *"Tout passe, tout lasse, tout casse"* -- badly translated as "everything passes, everything becomes tiresome, everything breaks." *Everything* includes anything that time renders irrelevant, including this unexceptional but candid work. I had no illusions about its utility or merit. But I kept going.

•

• •

I am indebted to my parents, learned, urbane, fair-minded and liberal, for instilling a love of books and an appreciation for music, art and philosophy, for sparing me the enslavement of religious indoctrination and for tolerating, if not always endorsing, my most reckless antics, some that nearly cost me my life, some that nearly bankrupted them. To my mother, a selfless, unassuming woman of great culture and refinement, I owe my love of beauty and symmetry. From my father, a loving, iron-willed and incorruptible man who abhorred ostentation and pretense, I learned that self-esteem and a respect for truth are far more important than other people's opinion.

I salute my teachers, in France, Romania and Israel. Their erudition, pedagogical skills and saintly patience for the lazy, unfocused, mercurial and rebellious student I was helped lay the foundation on which I would erect a lifetime career of endless beginnings and negligible achievements.

I can never fully assess the immense influence a number of prominent writers, poets and philosophers had on the person I would become. Their prose, verses and insights resonate as intensely today as they did in the days of my youth. Most were French; of these, one was denied a Christian funeral for his vitriolic anti-religious tracts; four were imprisoned, one for defying brutal colonial authorities in Indochina; the other for suggesting that the blind can be taught to read through the sense of touch; the third, the son of a prostitute, for vagabondage, lewd acts and "other offenses against public decency;" the fourth for stretching the limits of literary freedom in tracts that mixed raw eroticism and civil disobedience. The others wrote in English, German, Russian and Spanish. Three hailed from England; one of them did not survive the spurious morality of his Victorian milieu. All were freethinkers, rebels and idol smashers, now long dead, but whose works and the socially progressive ideas they impart continue to inspire new generations of readers and mavericks-in-training.

I offer heartfelt thanks to the many editors who overlooked my shortcomings and put up, at least for a while, with my eccentricities, incendiary style and overt penchant for rabble-rousing. They deserve a special accolade for teaching me, when they tired of me and consigned me to the far end of a long unemployment line, that "freedom of the press" extends as far as but not beyond the editor's desk and that it is generally reserved to those who own the presses.

"Without art," said George Bernard Shaw, *"the crudeness of reality would make the world unbearable."* This

maxim was driven home by my late maternal uncle Ionel, an art critic and author who fed my craving for esotericism and worked tirelessly to help refine my love of art. It was he who, after acquainting me with Giotto, Hals, Vermeer, Boucher, Kokoschka, Perahim and others, introduced me to Hieronymus Bosch. Poring over Bosch's paintings was like rummaging through a freshly unearthed time capsule. Once stripped of their surreal symbolism, as Ionel had taught me to do, his images leaped at me, bringing back memories of things I had seen before, not on the flat surface of a canvas or the pages of a picture book, but in the inescapable actuality of space-time where the crudeness of reality is further debased by the incivility of man. There was something familiar in Bosch's recurring scenes of sadism, the deadpan expressions of the evil-doers, the crushing sadness, the stunned fatalism in their quarries' faces. Familiar and terrifying. I would relive many heretofore repressed moments every time I gazed at his weird and often gruesome renderings of life and death. Captured through the prism of his age, his metaphors, I would realize, were ageless; their message was universal.

As far as I know, Hieronymus Bosch, who lashed out at superstition, not faith, is the only painter who had the genius and the temerity to juxtapose man's bestiality and the clergy's ceremonious stupor in the face of colossal human suffering. He ranks high in my pantheon of the world's great creative geniuses. He will never cease to fascinate me.

To my adored wife Linda, I reserve my deepest gratitude for her unequivocal love, her boundless generosity, her patience, her unflagging support of my wildest schemes, and for the untold concessions she continues to make along the way to grant me the luxury of being me.

BIBLIOGRAPHY

BEAGLE, Peter S. *The Garden of Earthly Delights*. The Viking Press, New York, 1982.

BERNSTEIN, Carl and **POLITI**, Marco, *His Holiness*. Random House, 1996.

BLOOM, Howard, *The Lucifer Principle*. Atlantic Monthly Press, 1995.

BURNS, Robert I. *Jews and Moors in the Siete Partidas of Alfonso X The Learned: a Background Perspective. Medieval Spain -- Culture, Conflict and Coexistence*, Edited by Roger Collins and Anthony Goodman, 2002.

CATHOLIC ENCYCLOPEDIA.

DAWKINS, Richard. *The God Delusion*. Houghton Mifflin, 2006

DE SADE, Donatien-Alphonse-François. *Justine.* Author's private collection.

DE TOLNAY, Charles. *Hieronymus Bosch*. Reynal & Co., New York, 1966.

DESCARTES, René. *Discours de la Méthode*. L'Intelligence. 1927. Limited edition.

DIDEROT, Denis. *Encyclopédie, 1759.*

DIRECTORIUM *Inquisitorium, 1578 edition*. Cornell University Collection, Ithaca, New York.

DOMINIQUE, Pierre. *L'Histoire des Papes*. Crapouillot, 1964.

ENCYCLOPEDIA BRITANICA.

ENCYCLOPEDIA JUDAICA.

FLEMYNG, Gordon. *Philby, Burgess and Maclean: Spy Scandal of the Century,* 1977.

FRIEDLANDER, Max J. and **CINOTTI,** Mia. *Jérôme Bosch.* Flammarion, Paris, 1967.

KAROLIDES, Nicholas J., **BALD,** Margaret, and **SOVA,** Dawn B. *120 Banned Books – Censorship Histories of World Literature.* Checkmark Books, 2005

LORD ACTON, *The Cambridge Modern History, Vol. I.* Cambridge University Press, 1910.

MANN, Horace K. *The Lives of the Popes in the Early Middle Ages, 1925.*

MCCABE, Dr. Joseph. *The Story of Religious Controversy.* 1929.

ORIENTI, Sandra and **DE SOLIER,** René. *Hieronymus Bosch – The Artist and His Time.* Siloe Editions, Paris, 1977.

PAGLEN, Trevor. *Blank Spots on the Map: The Dark Geography of the Pentagon's Secret World.* Dutton, 2009.

PANOFSKY, Erwin. *Studies in Iconology.* 1939.

SHORTO, Russell. Descartes' Bones: A Skeletal History of the Conflict Between Faith and Reason. Doubleday, 2008.

STANIC, Michael. *Jérôme Bosch -- Commentaire.* SACELP, Paris, 1986.

THE POPES, *A Concise Biographical History.* Edited by Eric John, 1994.

ABOUT THE AUTHOR

Born in Paris, educated in France, Romania and Israel, **W. E. Gutman** is a widely published veteran journalist. Between 1991 and 2006, he covered politics, the military, human rights and other socio-economic issues in Central America. Formerly the international editor of the futurist New York-based magazine, *OMNI*, and U.S. editor of the Moscow-based magazine, *Science in the USSR*, he continues to write for a number of mainstream and special-interest publications. A self-described iconoclast, devout atheist and Freemason, he lives with his wife in Southern California's "high desert."

www.ingramcontent.com/pod-product-compliance
Lightning Source LLC
Chambersburg PA
CBHW031119030726
47496CB00002BA/601

* 9 7 8 1 9 2 6 5 8 5 7 5 8 *